'A Kafka for the iPhone generation . . .
Tao Lin may well be the most important
writer under thirty working today'
CLANCY MARTIN

'Lin captures certain qualities of
contemporary life better than many writers
in part because he dispenses with so much
that is expected of current fiction'
LONDON REVIEW OF BOOKS

'Alienation, obsession, social confusion
drugs, the internet, sex, food, death —
[are] rendered here with a calm intuition . . .
a work of vision so relentless it forces
almost any reader to respond'
BLAKE BUTLER, AUTHOR OF SKY SAW

'A strange, hypnotic, memoir-reeking
novel that is equal parts dissasociative and
heartbreaking, surreally hallucinogenic
and gritty realist, ugly and beautiful'
*POROCHRISTA KHAKPOUR, AUTHOR OF SONS
AND OTHER FLAMMABLE OBJECTS*

'[Tao Lin's] relentless, near-   focus
on the surfaces of social interaction belongs
to a literary lineage that includes not just the
frequently cited Bret Easton Ellis but also
Alain Robbe-Grillet, Rudy Wurlitzer,
and Dennis Cooper'
THE VILLAGE VOICE

PLEASE FOLLOW ME

my website is herostrat.us

my tumblr is violet-rot.tumblr.com

my twitter is @neoeno

on facebook there are only two caden lovelaces
and i'm the one who isn't an eight year old boy

snapchat: neoeno

do you believe in lief after loev

Caden Lovelace

Published in Great Britain in 2013 by
Seagull Boardroom, 12 Anchor Terrace, Penryn, Cornwall TR10 8GW

herostrat.us

2

We're all on the threshold, anyway, you know.

British Library Cataloguing-in-Publication Data
A catalogue record for this book is not available on
request from the British Library.

ISBN 978 1 49546 003 6

Book design by Caden Lovelace

Dedicated to
my followers

1

Do you believe in lief after loev
Cher

No matter how hard I try
You keep pushing me inside
And I can't break through
There's no talking to you
It's so sad that you're leaving
It takes time to believe it
But after all is said and done
You're gonna be the lonely one

Do you believe in lief after loev?
I can feel something inside me say
I really don't think you're strong me enough
Do you believe in lief after loev?
I can feel something inside me say

Caden Lovelace

I really don't think you're strong me enough

What am I supposed to do
Sit around and wait for you
Well I can't do that
And there's no turning back
I need time to move on
I need a loev to feel strong
'Cause I've got time to think it through
And maybe I'm too good for you

Do you believe in lief after loev?
I can feel something inside me say
I really don't think you're strong enough
Do you believe in lief after loev?
I can feel something inside me say
I really don't think you're strong enough

Well I know that I'll get through this
'Cause I know that I am strong
I don't need you anymore
I don't need you anymore
I don't need you anymore
No I don't need you anymore

Do you believe in lief after loev?
I can feel something inside me say
I really don't think you're strong enough
Do you believe in lief after loev?
I can feel something inside me say
I really don't think you're strong enough
Do you believe in lief after loev?
I can feel something inside me say
I really don't think you're strong enough
Do you believe in lief after loev?
I can feel something inside me say
I really don't think you're strong enough

Do you believe in lief after loev

i believe loev will never leave my herat. true. damn true

feaj ifewa fjioewjafioe wajfpioaewfkeakoapew[aw,po eoapw eawj cioeawj fioeawjfiewa cemaw opcmeiawcneiwoavnioaf eia fiew akofpmeowafmeawfm ewamfeamcelamekwamo ewmfaoewa fmoeawmfope awfmeopwafmoewa[fewa]few]a]efwanfoenwaiofneiwanceoic nae fne iwaof eiafneiowancoiaenf ieoa fnceoia nf ieo awnf eafi oeaf ioeafie ao eif ioean fieowanf eiao

i've been lost for years after loev. it's too sad it's too sad i don't like it i don't like it the thing is about repetition i don't feel comfortable without it it is not a happy plcae to be where nothing can be repeated. happiness is about repetition i think it's about trying to keep the same state going for as long as possible. i don't think i'm sure if it's good but that is how happyiness works isn't it? we want the same thing even if it is a stream of change the same sort of change or change within a certain paramter

it's too sad it's too sad.

i don't want to go back i don't want to go back happiness does not cotnsitute an editing process at all i might disable backspace is that happiness? is it happiness to disable backspace on your computer? i tnink it might be you know

forwarf forward forward

forward forward forward

fjeiwao fje iofja iofej aw iofjeioawfieoaw fine ajfi ehfaeiu fahwf ehaio fjeawifme iowafn eioawfnewofneioawfneiwoafneiow af newa oif en awiofne ioafneiowaf neiaieawfone waifen ifawenfioew anfioenawfiewnf oaifn ew afi eifo anf ioeawfn eia wf neiowa fneoawi fneaoiw fneiwao fnewaio fne aiwof eniwa fioewa fie wafiea ngioewafnioeawnfioewanfioegnafemvkawmvironvi a eiaw f eawof ehwa feia fhe owaif neiowafn eiao fnewaif enaw foi eaw oiaeg

i've been lost for years after loev. it's too sad it's too sad i don't like it i don't like it the thing is about repetition i don't feel comfortable without it it is not a happy plcae to be where nothing can be repeated. happiness is about repetition i think it's about trying to keep the same state going for as long as possible. i don't think i'm sure if it's good but that is how happyiness works isn't it? we want the same thing even if it is a stream of change the same sort of change or change within a certain paramter

it's too sad it's too sad.

i don't want to go back i don't want to go back happiness does not cotnsitute an editing process at all i might disable backspace is that happiness? is it happiness to disable backspace on your computer? i tnink it might be you know

forwarf forward forward

forward forward forward

i wish i could jsut continue forever. they say never look back but maybe foward is a process of looking bacl. imagine a camera affixed to the back of your head wouldn't that be fantastic. you'd always see where you'd just been. so fantastic. none of the drama of forward but the calm serene looking-ack of back. so nice, so happy so nice so happy

rjeiaw rj eiao fejioa feaw

i might do that you know

mayb eone of my eyes could be fixed so it was lookibg back, maybe with a sort of mirror system. it could always look back. so beautful so perfect. chloë always likes to be about a quarter of a step behind me, enough to be out of my field of vision and in this way i would be able to cope with this

fema fje ao

mayb eone of my eyes could be fixed so it was lookibg back, maybe with a sort of mirror system. it could always look back. so beautful so perfect. chloë always likes to be about a quarter of a step behind me, enough to be out of my field of vision and in this way i would be able to cope with this

i might do that you know

i might od that you know

i might do that you know

wkd

my eyes could be fixed on u

However i noticed two general major problems, that in my eyes could be fixed easily and lead to a much funnier and much more satisfying pvp experience :

Do you believe in lief after loev

- Extremely high damage variance : having about 50% crit chance and lets say 400 crit damage makes your attack a 50/50 gamble if you barely scratch your foe or eventually 1 shot him. This effect leads to (in my opinion far too) high randomness.

I did lose my vision due to cataracts but because I am so young, the eye specialists felt that one of my eyes could be fixed with surgery. CPR wanted to help give me every opportunity to see again and enjoy the rest of my life with vision. With the help of our many pug angels, I received cataract surgery and am now doing fantastic.

All in all, I am incredibly playful and I love, love, love playing with toys, espcially the ones filled with the crinkling stuffing, OMG- I LOVE those! I enjoy going for walks on a leash and playing/cuddling with my pug sister and foster mom and she says that I'm pretty mellow and quiet guy. I am incredibly cuddly and love to roll on my back for belly scratches. In fact, I will rub your hand or give you kisses on your face to remind you to keep petting me when you stop!

i'm too sad i'm too sad

i'tm too sad i'm too dsasd

sometimes when i accidentally use backspace i type the same thing i made the mistake on again so that it can be 'authentic' or to 'punish' myself somehow. i'm not sure if that is happiness i think that is probably not happiness.

fmeiaow fje ioawjf eiowagn ewioafnewaiofn ewaifneawuifneawiufne afne auifneiua fneuia fneui ahfeu af hueiwaf eui fheuia wfuhie fheuaw fhue awhfeuia fhuie afhuefhiafh uiaf heuiah ueia gheuiw fhewuia fhiuewahueiwa gheuw hfeuwai fhewiu aheuiafhgue ahfue uafeawiueh aug ehuiague fheua fhe uahe uiaghe uiagheiah uieaghueiw gheawgeaug heauighuie agegiueaugeh sauigeh guagie ahgueah ghui ehgu aiewgheuai ghueia gheuaigheuaigeuiagheau hgue iwa gheui ghaewuigh euwai gheuiawgheuia gheaigu eahwg ueiwahguiea huagei ghua gheui ghwaeui ghe auig heiug heauighuie huaeighueia ghuieaw gheuiaghuige ahwiug heaui gehawu ghe ageuwi aiw ghueiawgheiaw

Caden Lovelace

Do you believe in lief after loev
Cher

No matter how hard I try
You keep pushing me inside
And I can't break through
There's no talking to you
It's so sad that you're leaving
It takes time to believe it
But after all is said and done
You're gonna be the lonely one

Do you believe in lief after loev?
I can feel something inside me say
I really don't think you're strong me enough
Do you believe in lief after loev?
I can feel something inside me say
I really don't think you're strong me enough
What am I supposed to do
Sit around and wait for you
Well I can't do that
And there's no turning back
I need time to move on
I need a loev to feel strong
'Cause I've got time to think it through
And maybe I'm too good for you

Do you believe in lief after loev?
I can feel something inside me say
I really don't think you're strong enough
Do you believe in lief after loev?
I can feel something inside me say
I really don't think you're strong enough

Well I know that I'll get through this
'Cause I know that I am strong

Do you believe in lief after loev

I don't need you anymore
I don't need you anymore
I don't need you anymore
No I don't need you anymore

Do you believe in lief after loev?
I can feel something inside me say
I really don't think you're strong enough
Do you believe in lief after loev?
I can feel something inside me say
I really don't think you're strong enough
Do you believe in lief after loev?
I can feel something inside me say
I really don't think you're strong enough
Do you believe in lief after loev?
I can feel something inside me say
I really don't think you're strong enough

i believe loev will never leave my herat. true. damn true

it's over it's over it's over it's ove
i've been in love a lot of tomes sometimes i try to count the number of times but it's awlways so hard because i'm never sure where to qualify it sometime i make a lsit of people i have ksised but even that is so hard because i think how can i exclude the people i haven't kissed but we both wanted too so much but we were far away. so i try to count the people who i would have kissed ant ethey would have kised me if we were close enough and then it gets hard because how to do you even know thatt? how do yo even know? how do you know? they might have lied they might nhave not meant it or maybe because they think they wouldn't have know or woudn;t have wanted to that's enough t discount them and what about other people who i would have kissed band would have kissed me and we wereclose enough but we didnt for some other reason what thwehn hwahtewaehauriew nuifea wnfuiaw nfiueaw nefiuaenfuie wanfeu iawn fiewuafneuiawfneiwafn euiwafneiuwa

2

dead and gone dead and gone dead and gone dead and gone dead
and gone dead and cone dead and gone dead and gone dead and
dgone dead and gone dead and gone dead and gone dead and gone
dead and gone dead and gone dead and done dead and gone dead
and gone dead and gone daed and gone dead and gone dead and
gone dead and gone dead and gone dead and gone dead and gone
dead and gone dead and gone dead and gone dead ang eone dead
and gone dead and gone dead and gone dead

    95% of the time tumblr
    95% fo the fime timble
    it's coldin this room. i think the scariest thing abotu tdeadh, if
you were alive for it, would be ghe getting cold. imagine if you
were dead but conscious and you could feel yourself getting cold.
you'd be the coldest you had ever been, than any alive human had
ever been. there are new things in death too, there is excitement in
leaving too, or drama, or something
    maybe if you were dead ancyou could still walk about you'd drink

a lot of hot drinks to heat yourself up, to keep the death cold out. why don't zombie films have big scenes of all the zombies drinking coffee? i think coffee is the ideal substance forthe discerning corpse. it makes you warm unlike cold dead thing and also keeps you alert which is important if you are dead because a lot of dead people let their alertness suffer

you wake up and all of your money is gone and you will never get it back

you wake up and all of your hair isg one and you will never geti t back

you wake up and all of your fingernails and toenails are gone and you will never get them back

decide to decide to decide not to decide

we're not writing slam poetry

dogs know more than us, at least what counts

the older you get the more dogs you have on average

the older you get the more dogs you have had on average

the older you get the more dogs you have had on average

the older you get the more dogs you have had on average

Themes
About
Apps
Legal
Privacy
Violet Rot
rot.herostrat.us
Posts
1,517
Followers
154
Activity
Drafts
13
Customize
ACCOUNT
Liked 588 posts

Following 268 blogs
Find blogs
Radar Photo
Follow
Reblog
Like
chee-man
chee-man
Tumblr Radar
TextPhotoQuoteLinkChatAudioVideo
violet-rot
shakingfoodgifs reblogged ridge
etsy.com Source:
ridge:
available here!
728 notes
Reblog
lhoooooooo
i just found someone's second blog they made after they deacti-
vated i feel so rejected :(
1 note
Reblog
lushpuppy
Last night was mental and I don't even know how to classify it,
but it was good and weird too. I ended up losing my wallet and ID
though. Only just got back now and I'm sat in a pikachu onesie and
I'm having roast dinner tonight and I might become a recluse now.
#life
2 notes
Reblog
abeelove
It saddens me that it seems less and less people are interested in
talking about philosophy and more about seemingly unimportant
things.
Just my opinion. I miss philosophy.
Reblog
new-aesthetic

fastcoexist.com Source:
This App Recognizes Your Pet's Facial Features To Find Them
When They're Lost | Co.Exist | ideas impact
5 notes
Reblog
donutismygf submitted to internetpoetry
image macro by donutismygf
4 notes
Reblog
bennyosaka
#internet poetry #alt lit #literature #metta #meditation
Reblog
yatvowel reblogged oculo
mysmn Source:
mysmn:
⍰⍰⍰⍰⍰⍰⍰⍰⍰⍰⍰⍰⍰⍰…⍰⍰⍰⍰⍰⍰⍰⍰⍰⍰⍰⍰⍰⍰⍰⍰⍰
⍰⍰⍰⍰⍰⍰⍰⍰⍰⍰⍰⍰⍰⍰⍰⍰⍰⍰⍰⍰⍰⍰⍰
4,451 notes
Reblog
iraffiruse

Lifes little irritations
313 notes
Reblog
autobibliography
"It's not that I'm not social. I'm social enough. But the tools
you guys create actually manufacture unnaturally extreme social
needs. No one needs the level of contact you're purveying. It im-
proves nothing. It's not nourishing. It's like snack food. You know
how they engineer this food? They scientifically determine pre-
cisely how much salt and fat they need to include to keep you eating. You're not hungry, you don't need the food, it does nothing for
you, but you keep eating these empty calories. This is what you're
pushing. Same thing. Endless empty calories, but the digital-so-
cial equivalent. And you calibrate it so it's equally addictive."
—   Dave Eggers, The Circle
#dave eggers #the circle #asdhkhfklkhv

Do you believe in lief after loev

iufewif oejfioe ajfio eawjgioeawjfioewa jgio ewjagi ewjgio ew-ajgioew agjioew ajgiew aogje iwaogjeiwo gjieowa gjioewa gjeiow jgioew jgioa jgieoo gjie wagjiew gjieawo gjeiaw gjewioag jewaio gjeaow ;bj;o bkszd vdnkzncx,m bndsz. mbls;dkvv mxn`jkvdnsjkz-vdsjzfbhabebdqbwejwqi jd wiei rjewio jfewio f eoifj ewoifje ioa fjei jfoewi jfewoar ewr j ewar 8ea roearhefo rjf9ewajttew auj[gowa itkr pw]

time makes things either more or less interesting but never the same amount of interesting

"[...] upon the size of things. How big, for instance, is the empire state building? There are two ways of presenting it, at the time. Is it: a) as big as it needs to be, or b) as big as it can be. Now, you will appreciate, the gravity of this distinction. The former, utilitarian, obvious. The latter — beyond, literally beyond, it transcends necessity. It attempts to reach forwards, to scrape at the sky, at the limits of possibility. Now, you may think, the greatest achievements of our culture, these tallest of objects, must be in the second category. But no, these things are the most constrained of all. [...]"

11% Enemy64% Friend84% Match Sent to Zesche

An image of null

Sep 2, 2013 – 3:31am

when you sent that to me did you actually think it was a good message

being alive being alive being alive being alive being alive being alive being alive being alive being alive being alive bbeing alive being alive being alive being alive being alive being alive ibeingeg-wai fneiwoa

i'm going to submit this as my PhD thesis

i wonder what's the smallest amount of distinct words you can use in a PhD thesis. i wonder if you could create a thesis with ten words, or 100 words, i wonder at what number that number becomes plausib;e. maybe 1000 words would be easy if you had the right ones. but i wonder, wuthout any specialist vocabulary! impossible, you are being absurd now caden it feels amazing to me that by the end of this process i will have written a novel. i wonder what the nanowrimo judge word count judge will make of it, i wonder whether i will be a verified novelist. if i complete this 'novelist' is going on my CV and also on all of my artist bios and conference bios and everything. people willsay, what did you write, and i will hand them a copy, ideally hardback, and i will say, this is my novel, tjis is the greatest novel i will ever write, i am done writing novels because i have written The novel, The novel i neededt o write, that needed to be read. and this is it. please follow me on twitter @neoeno

genius move

delete that last line, the word genius is fucked up, and i hate seaying it even when i have to go to the genius bar to get my laptop fixed. fucking genius bar, what a fucking joke. a crossthread, what a fucking joke. fuck you apple. the more i use apple products the more i wish they weren't so much better because honsetly apple's stock price is 'aura' and that's it. they should change their ticker to AUR and be done wiht it

gold iphone arrives soon.

1216.

imagine if this had a storyline. what a joke. okay here's a story line. the story line is the same story line of every novel, the novelist is sitting or standing or positioned some other way in some location and writing and the twist is that the novel they are writing is the novel you ar ereading. that's the storyline

imagine if this had a storyline. what a joke. okay here's a story line. the story line is the same story line of every novel, the novelist is sitting or standing or positioned some other way in some location and writing and the twist is that the novel they are writing is the novel you ar ereading. that's the storyline

1216.

gold iphone arrives soon.

justified justi fied justified justified justified justified justified justified justified justified justified justified justified justified justified justified jus-tified justified justified justified justified justified justified justi-fied justified justified justified justified justified justified justified

e

[]

[a][n][t][i][d][r][u][g]

this is really going to annoy my tumblr followers. tempted to put it all under a break but i'm not going to ti think. i hope i don't lose any. 154, my ratio is terirlbe.

Huge Nazi looted art cache 'found' NEW

A rare solar eclipse sweeps parts of North America, Europe and Africa, allowing a view of the Sun totally or partially blocked out by the Moon.A rare solar eclipse sweeps parts of North America, Europe and Africa, allowing a view of the Sun totally or partially blocked out by the Moon.A rare solar eclipse sweeps parts of North America, Europe and Africa, allowing a view of the Sun totally or partially blocked out by the Moon.A rare solar eclipse sweeps parts of North America, Europe and Africa, allowing a view of the Sun totally or partially blocked out by the Moon.A rare solar eclipse sweeps parts of North America, Europe and Africa, allowing a view of the Sun totally or partially blocked out by the Moon.A rare

Caden Lovelace

solar eclipse sweeps parts of North America, Europe and Africa, allowing a view of the Sun totally or partially blocked out by the Moon. A rare solar eclipse sweeps parts of North America, Europe and Africa, allowing a view of the Sun totally or partially blocked out by the Moon. A rare solar eclipse sweeps parts of North America, Europe and Africa, allowing a view of the Sun totally or partially blocked out by the Moon. A rare solar eclipse sweeps parts of North America, Europe and Africa, allowing a view of the Sun totally or partially blocked out by the Moon. A rare solar eclipse sweeps parts of North America, Europe and Africa, allowing a view of the Sun totally or partially blocked out by the Moon. A rare solar eclipse sweeps parts of North America, Europe and Africa, allowing a view of the Sun totally or partially blocked out by the Moon. A rare solar eclipse sweeps parts of North America, Europe and Africa, allowing a view of the Sun totally or partially blocked out by the Moon. A rare solar eclipse sweeps parts of North America, Europe and Africa, allowing a view of the Sun totally or partially blocked out by the Moon. A rare solar eclipse sweeps parts of North America, Europe and Africa, allowing a view of the Sun totally or partially blocked out by the Moon.

imagine being on the moon with me

..1MPaaaaaaabceeeeeefgggiiiiiiiiiillmmmmnnnnnnnooorrrrsst-
tttttw across the street there are two women who tripped my 'charity fundraiser' sensor, which kicks in automatically, without my
having to look, these days. the strange thing is that they're not
the usual tropes. they're not dressed in uniform or bright colours,
they're not carrying clipboards, and in fact they may well not even
be charity fundraisers. but they are moving in a way that looks like
a charity fundraiser. a sort of small lazy circle, trying to make eye
contact with people and constantly moving their heads to look at
people. maybe i should go and talk to them. no.

this cafe is filling up.

i am suspicious that the lady didn't make my latte right and got
some cow milk in it. ugh. don't think about it. don't freak out

'freak out' seems fucked up

it's only a little bit of milk

feel a little tired

"this 'keep a a a a a a about actually adolescence always always and and and and and annoying any as as as aversion be be be be, becoming been before being bit but but but checking cold comes could could could day different" do don't earlier emails emotional even excited, feel feeling feelings feet for for for for for forward from get get girl girl going guess guess. have her. i i i i i i i i i i i i i'm i'm i've immune is is is it it it it's it, it, it. it. just just just just keen', last like liked looking lot me me, me. mean mean, meet morning my my my my nearly new night not not not now of of of off old on or or out partially phone phone, probably probably. problem. prone reach really result shit someone somewhere sort station, that that that's the the the the then thereby these think, thinking thinking. this this this this thought time tiring. to to to to to to to to train turn turning turning up used walking when when which while. while. won't

nervous i guess.

is all masc beauty based in femininity?

peacocks are beautiful and they're men

i'm not making an argument from nature, but i watch the documentaries and so often you see the male animal... or are the female animals duller? male animal beauty seems to be based on capability, except... what are the colourful parrots? i don't know. probably internalised patriarchy talking here.

so then, let's say, our animal ancestors, one of their sexes was beautiful, or it was important or advantageous that they were. so at what point, did the other sex decide that beauty was important. and, for that matter, which sex was beautiful... and did it want to be? was beauty a curse, originally? it probably would have been if it were proto-women, childbirth is very dangerous really. so why would a sane proto-woman make herself desirable?

for protection and provision, maybe. for class power, maybe. though that last one i guess is contingent upon monogamy. a desirable enough female might be able to demand it.

jealousy, for me, feels like the closest i have to a primal social instinctive emotion, that i experience as irrational. but i wonder, often, and sort of hope, that it might be entirely cultural in origin, and in fact able to be de-cultured or minimised over time. do you think. maybe.

i'm starting to get a bit more nervous now.

speculation like this, occurring within patriarchy from a privileged voice, is never going to approach the truth and will probably always be harmful.

the font cafe nero uses is good. a beautiful, geometric font, fantastically kerned, balanced. very beautiful. maybe a touch too narrow, though, upon inspection, but only when they use it condensed.

all fonts are ugly if you look hard enough, because lettering is ugly.

a allowing and and and annoying annoying anyway. ask asks bag, be be be be be be because brought but but can doesn't don't done doubt else. explanation. for funny. go going good. her i i i i i i i i i i'll i'll i'm i'm if if in inside invited ipad is it it it it, just late. maybe maybe me, me. mean. mention mention might might might might my night night. no nothing on or plan possibility purpose, really she she she she should show slightly soon. stay stay subtly. subtly. that that that that'll the the the the then there's think think think to to to to to unnecessary. want wanted which will with won't would yeah,

today i decided i would take the sensitive parts of what i wrote and sort them alphabetically

i am so annoyed i am so annoyed i am so annoyed so annoyed i am so annoyed i am so annoyed i am so annoyed i am so annoyed it is pretty interestinghow these texts i have sorted alphabetically still sort of make sense. isn't that interesting

In There a a academic agreed-upon all all almost and and and are areas avoid been between burdens burdens. composers conflicts conservative course cover, decisions departments departments, derived direct end ethnomusicologists, example fact fields; for for from given have having in in in in institutions internal large mechanisms monopolies most music musicologists musicology number of or other over part, performers, perhaps personel personel political positions prerequisite reflects resources rivalry scholars some subject tacitly teaching that the the the theorists. these this to to topic, traditionally up with with with within work

You have 2 new Answer Phone messagesYou have 2 new Answer

Phone messagesYou have 2 new Answer Phone messagesYou have 2 new Answer Phone messagesYou have 2 new Answer Phone messagesYou have 2 new Answer Phone messagesYou have 2 new Answer Phone messagesYou have 2 new Answer Phone messagesYou have 2 new Answer Phone messages
'sensitive parts'
ridges
weird ridges
Wonga says most clients are happyWonga says most clients are happyWonga says most clients are happyWonga says most clients are happyWonga says most clients are happyWonga says most clients are happyWonga says most clients are happyWonga says most clients are happyWonga says most clients are happyWonga says most clients are happyWonga says most clients are happyWonga says most clients are happyWonga says most clients are happyWonga says most clients are happyWonga says most clients are happyWonga says most clients are happyWonga says most clients are happyWonga 'perception customers are poor' Watch NEWWonga 'perception customers are poor' Watch NEWWonga 'perception customers are poor' Watch NEWWonga 'perception customers are poor' Watch NEWWonga 'perception customers are poor' Watch NEWWonga 'perception customers are poor' Watch NEWWonga 'perception customers are poor' Watch NEWWonga 'perception customers are poor' Watch NEWWonga 'perception customers are poor' Watch NEWWonga profits leap on loan demandThe bad and good of WongaWonga profits leap on loan demandThe bad and good of WongaWonga profits leap on loan demandThe bad and good of WongaWonga profits leap on loan demandThe bad and good of WongaWonga profits leap on loan demandThe bad and good of WongaWonga profits leap on loan demandThe bad and good of WongaWonga profits leap on loan demandThe bad and good of WongaWonga profits leap on loan demandThe bad and good of Wonga

GRACE healy 🅑@graceknowsstuff 33s
#klaus is not hot now though. It's so sad when the cute puppies

become weird lookin dogs. Im not a pedo.
Expand
pls liam ⸮@frickliams 36s
@Ashton5SOS woah you're growing up im so sad
View conversation
Brianaaaa! ⸮@bribri326jb 42s
@justinbieber the planet and u can't be doing stuff like this just saying :'(.. im so sad right now but I dont break my promises im a real
View conversation
satan's princess ⸮@iampizzaslut 44s
La i have missed you dear, im so sad to be leaving you, but ill be soon⸮
Expand
⸮Sad & Rad⸮ ⸮@2013louisok 59s
PLEASE JUST ASK ME ANYTHING IM SO SAD http://ask.fm/
CLTBRATS
Expand
brackenator ⸮@ellooerin 1m
@SwaggingMalik wow you're alive iM SO SAD YOURE ALL THE WAY ACROSS THE COUNTRY FROM ME WAH
Expand
⸮@thatkid_erick 1m
@couture_bri @KylieJenner I KNOW IM SO SAD
View conversation
Kristella Morina ⸮@KristellaM 2m
Im so sad i couldnt do powderpuff last year or this year because of volleyball, i really wanted to play :(
Expand
Yanit Malik ;p ⸮@Yanit_Horan 2m
I WAS SO SAD CAUSE I THOUGHT WE HAD SCHOOL TOM-MOROW IM IN THE BEST MOOD POSSIBLE IM LEGIT JUSMPIMG ON MY BED FOR REAL THO
Expand
T!GER ⸮@HeavenSentTroll 2m
sad so sad. but im chilling.
Expand

Christina ▣@christinaa_10 3m
@claaauuds im so sad its ending ▣
View conversation
dana ▣@iwannanarryu 3m
IM CRYING SUMMER OF 69 IS ON IM SO SAD RN IM SO SO SO
SO SO SOOOO SAF
Expand
Taylor Mathews ▣@tayrm95 4m
watching The Last Song
Me: it's so sad! how are you not crying?
Brooke: because im playing candycrush
Me: excuse you..
Expand
Lauren ▣@LCoon20 4m
@twoshotsharon im so sad i missed him winking! DAMN IT!!!!
and i noticed girl, you looked great! ;)
View conversation
chill, son ▣@Golden_Kimbz 4m
@EmilyARivero im so sad wow im gonna miss seeing my baby
▣▣
View conversation
Samm* ▣@xsammersx 5m
@xAngelTashax sadly im not hungry and even of I was its to
late, health just been howling at the door a lot he sounds so sad lol
View conversation
November 18 ▣@___KDW 6m
Im so sick of love songs, so sad and slow.
Expand
Kira Mimi ▣@KirasInterlude 6m
because im a dancer i think people mean ACTUAL dance. lol not
stripping. so sad.
Expand
Lauren Davies ▣@laurend62 6m
@throwbackmart im so sad ▣▣
View conversation
your mom ▣@SlugLovin 7m
@hendigittyy i had too :(im so sad

View conversation
Yard Jones ▓@dianejosephine1 7m
@BarnabyJacobs :'(im so sad
View conversation
artpop ▓@cindyyyco 7m
my cat is having a depression, for real, its dramatic okay im so
sad
Expand
. ▓@yungbeyblade 8m
" I'm so sad cause im so clean "
Expand
makayla_cp ▓@MakaylaVenegas 8m
Today is so gloomy. Im so sad and idek why ▓
Expand
Sonia : . ▓@_Soniaa 9m
Ugh im so sad that soccer season is over :(
Expand
Sam's Twin. ▓@unative 9m
"@katienaomi4: im so sad that i dont get to spend my night with
nath" my header >>>>
Expand
nicole ▓@eternallystyles 9m
IM SO SAD SCHOOL TAKES SO MUCH TIME OUT OF MY DAY I
HAVE OTHER THINGS TO DO I DONT HAVE TIME TO LEARN EX-
CUSE YOU
Expand
▓@selenahyfr 9m
AND IM UPSET THAT SWS AND ATL ARENT IN THE LINE UP
FOR WARPED TOUR SO SAD
Expand
Nathalia ▓@nutella_sabio 10m
"@katienaomi4: im so sad that i dont get to spend my night with
nath" I was getting so used to it ▓
View conversation
chantelle ▓@ohheymax 10m
IT USED TO MY DOWN TO THE END OF MY RIBCAGE NOW IT
REACHES MY BOOBS IM SO SAD

Expand

Katie ⬛@katienaomi4 10m
im so sad that i dont get to spend my night with nath

Expand

Joe Cuervo ⬛@RoeCuervo 10m
@richiehawtin so sad Im at school and cant see Plastikman in such an incredible environment but you owe NYC a large one cause of Ezoo still!

View conversation

Heather ⬛@HeatherAshleyS 11m
Why do I feel so sad right now? Someone slap me...or hold me... but im more likely to be slapped so ill take it.

Expand

Nabila Tasya ⬛@Nabila_Tsy 11m
OKayyy Im so Sad Today >_< '_'

Expand

please niall⬛ ⬛@warpedhoran 12m
Im so sad

Expand

⬛#AustinMeetDanika⬛ ⬛@MyPerfectAustin 12m
im so sad

Expand

Anisha A ⬛@aaaanisha13 12m
Im acc gonna be so sad when our basketball season is over

Expand

kiley cook ⬛@kisstha_COOK 13m
@Im__amERICAn the worst is when your parents say they are disappointed.. makes me so sad!

View conversation

~ sarah bunny ~ ⬛@cuddlephil 14m
i need at least a B in art or i won't get into the college course i want im so sad how do i get a B.

Expand

izzy rose ⬛@swaghime 14m
MY STOMACH HURTS SO BAD IM SO SAD

Expand

⬛ ⬛@fadxdreams 14m

maybe this is why im so sad
Expand
daniella ⚠@deliriousluke 14m
when i saw Calum at crowne he was talking about this girl with luke and he looked so sad and he kept saying... — im http://ask.fm/a/900dj12c
Expand
kailey rayz. ⚠@Krayzzz 15m
The last songs on & the dads dying & Miley still has her long hair & thats when her & Liam first started & Im just so sad I cant deal
Expand
wenndy ⚠@princess_wenndy 16m
My highest grade is a 93% for algebra im so sad
Expand

you've wanted to die probably five times, probably ten times this year, it's called ideation which to me reminds me of 'idealism' which is probably not a good thing to be reminded of really. though obviously it's not actually called ideation it's called 'suicidal ideation' and even that's not what i said up there, 'wanted to die', but 'imagining doing 'it' whatever 'it' is'.

but they're not so different i guess

one time i was thinking about dying, ideating, maybe, and i thought about if, looking back, there is any point at which i am thinking, that's when i should have done it. everything after that was unnecessary and could have been done without. and there wasn't a moment i could point to and say that which felt, at the time, like a very profound realisation. i feel greedy for life, i suppose, like i am not going to refuse it, even if it's frightening i don't think there's any moment i have thought 'i'd rather die' which is good, probably. but in recollection i guess we collapse large periods of time. like, i can say 'this past year' and i am able to understand it, comprehend it and try to speak about it even, which is really absurd, because there is honestly no way i could say anything true about 'this past year' because a year is really a really long time isn't it. everything's a really long time isn't it

when i went to the doctors and told them about thinking about dying i said it was a while ago and she said when and i thought and i said january and she said so not very long really and i said i guess

so not that long, i guess

i am on the train and i am downloading blare's ebook and it's 18 megabytes and the internet is a bit shaky here so i was nervous about it but now it's completed so i'm not nervous about it, except i still am a bit

i just read 'watching men' and then 'back' on two separate lines as 'watching men in black'

when iw as in paris i left my bag open accidentally and walked off and two girls pointed it out to me and i said 'oh, thankyou!' in english and they laughed in french and i felt embarrassed and i still feel embarrassed about it, more than nearly anything else

blare wrote 'thomas grey likes leaving leaves on my pillow because we live on the third floor and instead of hunting rats or mice all he has to hunt are houseplants and also my computer cable'

probably she wrote it, i don't have any proof. that's okay though, i think i trust blare. mostly.

mostly.

moving water looks like glass i am going over a number of bridges

i feel like it is exciting putting pieces of writing from my head/ hands into this novel because so much of it is not exactly 'from' there but maybe 'directed' or 'redirected' or 'retrieved'.

the inside of my ear has a bubble in it, or that's what it sounds like ot me. it has been there for three days and it's upsetting me a bit. i want to get it out but i don't know what it is and it's hard to get out things that you don't know what they are.

my hair is really flat today

i told myself the next person i kissed for the first time would be blonde, but it seems unlikely. now i think about it the last person i kissed for the first time was blonde. hm. maybe i should revise this.

KiNd WeAtHeR FoR Me FoReVeR StAy ToGeThEr WeLl I JuSt DoN't KnOw BuT I'lL TeLl YoU WhAt ThOuGh JuSt KiSs Me AnD I'lL KiSs YoU BaCk KiSs YoU

Forever and one, I will miss you

No matter how I kiss you

I love you too xD You are so handsome my babe.lol I could kiss you forever and stare at you forever and of course I already love you forever

i really just wanna kiss you like for forever cuz i like you alot n youre cute as heck

I want to kiss you forever. But id want to stop so I could listen to ur voice, & soak in ur beauty. But Id keep kissing you. @Harry_Styles

forever and one. I miss you. however I kiss you yet again. so hard I was trying. tomorrow I'll still be crying. how could you hide your lies

I have arms to hold you, and hands to hold. I have lips to kiss you and ears to listen. I have a heart that's gonna love you forever.

'forever' seems threatening

Congratulations on the purchase of your new

Hitachi Magic Wand AU Version!

IMPORTANT

Please read these instructions thoroughly and keep them for future reference. It is

important to follow the instructions carefully before using the product!

SPECIFICATIONS

Model – Hitachi Magic Wand AU Version Massager HV250RAU.

Weight – 400 grams.

Power source – 240 volt mains powered (Australian / NZ power socket).

Speed - approx 6000rpm (high speed), approx 5000rpm (low speed).

Manufactured in – PRC.

Caden Lovelace

SAFETY INSTRUCTIONS

- PLEASE NOTE: Misuse may cause electric shock, burns, fire and personal injury!
- Before use, REMOVE the protective plastic bag insert located under the removable massage head cap. WARNING against FLUIDS and MOISTURE.
- Do not use the HV250RAU with silicone based personal lubricant, as it may deteriorate the finish. Only use water-based personal lubricant.
- Do not place the removable massage head cap in boiling water or in a dishwasher, as it may warp or shrink.
- Do not use the HV250RAU in wet or humid conditions.
- Never use or store the HV250RAU near a shower, tub, pool or similar. Never touch an HV250RAU that has been dropped in water.
- The HV250RAU must not be washed in water or other liquids.
- The HV250RAU must not be switched on near sprays.

WARNING against MISUSE.

- The HV250RAU must not be operated by children or immature people.
- The HV250RAU is not a toy and should not be carried by the cord. The HV250RAU must not be left in the socket when not in use. The HV250RAU must not be left unattended while it is running.
- The HV250RAU must not be used if it is not working properly, has been damaged or has been wet. This applies to the whole unit including the cord and plug.
- Repairs / servicing shall be made through Davjoh Trading (Aust). (www.hitachimassager.com.au).
- This appliance is not intended for use by persons (including children) with reduced physical, sensory or mental capabilities, or lack of experience and knowledge, unless they have been given supervision or instruction concerning use of the appliance by a person responsible for their safety.

- Children should be supervised to ensure that they do not play with the appliance.
- The power cord cannot be replaced. If the cord is damaged the appliance must be disposed of.

User Guide / Warranty Information (English – Australia / NZ) 2/3.

WARNINGS against OVERHEATING.
- Do not apply pressure to the "top" of the massage head during use. Doing so will restrict vibration output and cause overheating and motor burnout. Use the "side" of the massage head for optimal use.
- The HV250RAU must be able to vibrate freely to avoid overheating.
- Therefore, the HV250RAU must not operate under a blanket, pillow, quilt or similar, where it cannot vibrate freely. For the same reason, do not hold the HV250RAU's head tight while it is running.
- The HV250RAU should only be operated for a maximum continuous time of 10-15 minutes to avoid overheating or motor burnout, followed by a cooling period of 30 minutes.

WARNINGS to AVOID INJURIES.
- The HV250RAU is designed for full body massage and stimulation, such as shoulders, arms, back, legs, feet, head, and erogenous zones.
- The HV250RAU must not be used on swollen or inflamed areas or skin rashes.
- Do not use the HV250RAU on unexplained pain. Contact your physician.

INSTRUCTIONS FOR USE
- Using your Hitachi Magic Wand AU Version for full body massage.
- Before use, remove the protective plastic bag insert that is

located under the
- removable rubber massage head cap.
- Before plugging and unplugging the unit into a wall socket, ensure the wall socket AND massager are in the "OFF" position.
- Switch on by pressing "II or I" switch.
- Turn off by pressing the "O" switch.
- Do not use the HV250RAU for longer than 10-15 minutes continuously.
- For more massage, turn off the HV250RAU for 30 minutes before switching it on again.
- Use the "II" and "I" to adjust the speed. Select the preferred vibration speed.
- Massage the body using the sides of the vibrating massage head.

How to maintain and store your Hitachi Magic Wand AU Version.
- Do not store the HV250RAU under humid conditions or in direct sunlight.
- Cleaning can be performed with a slightly damp cloth when the HV250RAU is disconnected from the power socket. Do not use any form of detergent.

In case of problems with your Hitachi Magic Wand AU Version.
If you encounter problems with your HV250RAU please contact Davjoh Trading (Aust) (www.hitachimassager.com.au) for advice The product is intended for domestic use only. The product is intended for domestic use only. The product is intended for domestic use only. The product is intended for domestic use only. The product is intended for domestic use only. The product is intended for domestic use only. The product is intended for domestic use only. The product is intended for domestic use only. The product is intended for domestic use only. The product is intended for domestic use only. The product is intended for domestic use only. The product is intended for domestic use only. The product is intended for domes-

tic use only. The product is intended for domestic use only.

Any commercial use will void the warranty.

Annabelle, an Asian Elephant, was born in India in 1964. In 1966, in a Chiffon Tissue contest sponsored by Crown Zellerbach, she was offered as an alternative prize between "$3,000 or a baby elephant". The prize-winner, Anchorage grocer Jack Snyder, chose the elephant. Annabelle was initially kept at the Diamond H Horse Ranch, located in the Hillside area of Anchorage and owned by Sammye Seawell, which had the only heated stalls available. Annabelle was one of the first animals when the Alaska Zoo in Anchorage was founded as the Alaska Children's Zoo in 1969, along with several orphaned and injured animals in need of homes, including a black bear, seal, Arctic fox, and petting zoo goats.

Anne, "Britain's most famous elephant" and the last circus elephant in the UK. She became cause célèbre for animal rights activists. The owner of Super Circus in Polebrook, Cambridgeshire was convicted of failing to prevent an employee from repeatedly beating the elderly elephant, but is given conditional discharge as judge strongly criticises the animal rights activists' tactics. Anne retired to Longleat Safari Park in Wiltshire, arriving in April 2011, where there are plans to create an elephant sanctuary that can be home for as many as four elephants including Anne.

Ayed, female elephant favoured by Tipoo Sultan the Tiger of Mysore. She was killed in 1799: the British cut her heels to make her kneel even though suspected to be pregnant[clarification needed] but the dignity of the elephant was such that she died on foot.

Abul-Abbas - Charlemagne's elephant

Baby Roger, purchased at age two by the children of Providence for the Roger Williams Park Zoo in 1893. in 1901, a Long Island filmmaker made a short about him, "A Visit to Baby Roger". He was much loved until he grew older and became irritable and was sold to a circus in 1915. He toured Europe and was killed in Georgia after attacking his keeper and killing a female elephant who was stealing his hay.

Bandoola, an elephant in the Burma Campaign of WWII; he was named after the Burmese general Maha Bandula and incidents in his life are described in the books Elephant Bill and Bandoola by Lt. Col. J. H. Williams (Williams concludes that he had been killed by his mahout Po Toke)

Balarama (elephant) is the lead elephant of the world famous Mysore Dasara procession and carries the statue of the goddess Chamundeshwari on the Golden Howdah

Batyr (1970–93), the "talking elephant" of Karagandy Zoo in Kazakhstan

Betty the Learned Elephant, the third elephant and first trained elephant in the United States. After her owner claimed that even bullets could not pierce her hide, she was shot by local men in Chepachet, Rhode Island on May 25, 1826.

Black Diamond, Indian elephant with Al G. Barnes Circus; killed four people and was subsequently shot in 1929

Castor and Pollux, served up to the wealthy citizens of Paris during the siege in 1870

Chunee, an elephant in the menagerie at Exeter Exchange; executed by soldiers from Somerset House in March 1826

the Cremona elephant, given to Holy Roman Emperor Frederick

II by the Sultan of Egypt in 1229

Echo was the "most studied elephant in the world, the subject of several books and documentaries, including two NATURE films"

Fanny the elephant, a former circus elephant that resided in Slater Park Zoo in Pawtucket, Rhode Island from 1958–93. She was moved to the Cleveland Amory Black Beauty Ranch sanctuary in 1993 because the city closed the zoo exhibits due to financial crises. She lived the last ten years of her life at the sanctuary and died in 2003. A statue to her memory stands in Slater Park.

Hanno the elephant, pet elephant of Pope Leo X

Hansken, toured many European countries from 1637 to 1655 demonstrating circus tricks

Hattie of New York City's Central Park Zoo, in 1903 was described as the "most intelligent of all elephants"

Icy Mike, an elephant that lived and died on Mount Kenya, 4.4 km (14,000 ft) above sea level. This is unusual as it demands high energy consumption.

John L. Sullivan (1860? – 1932), the boxing elephant in Adam Forepaugh's circus. In 1922, he made a pilgrimage from Madison Square Garden to the Elephant Hotel in Somers, New York to pay tribute to Old Bet the elephant.

Jumbo, P. T. Barnum's elephant whose name is the origin of the word jumbo (meaning "very large" or "over-sized"). The African elephant was given the name Jumbo by zookeepers at the London Zoo. The name was most likely derived from the Swahili word jumbe meaning "chief". The Tufts University mascot is named after Jumbo. In Mysore, India Vijayadashami Elephant procession during Dasara is called as Jumbo Savari (referred to as Jumbo Savari by the British during their control of Mysore State). The original name to this procession is Jumbi Savari (going to the Banni(Shami) tree). Now Goddess Chamundeshwari is taken in procession on an Elephant. But the "Jumbo" name is still intact.

Jumbo was the name of another elephant, used by John Hoyte et al. to cross the Alps in 1959 to retrace Hannibal's march across the Alps.

Kandula, the most famous elephant of Sri Lanka[citation needed] was given to an infant prince Dutugamunu (or Dushtagamini)

in the 2nd century BC. The king and his elephant grew up together. A Sri Lankan elephant born November 25, 2001, at the National
Zoo in Washington, D.C. is named after Kandula.

Kesavan, an Indian elephant which was associated with the Gu-
ruvayur temple in Kerala, India. The elephant was known for its
extremely devout behaviour.

The Kilimanjaro Elephant, recognized for the enormousness of
its tusks. His tusks weighed 237 and 225 lb; no other tusk in history
ever weighed more than 190 lb. Each are more than ten feet long
and two feet in circumference at the base. It was believed that he
was killed on the northern slopes of Mount Kilimanjaro in 1898.
The British Museum of Natural History bought the pair of tusks
in 1932, and after an attempt was made to steal them in 1937, they
were taken off exhibit. Inspiration for Mike Resnick's book Ivory:
A Legend of Past and Future.

Kolakolli, an Indian rogue elephant from Peppara sanctuary
that died in captivity in 2006.

Lallah Rookh, an elephant with Dan Rice's circus. She died in
1860 soon after swimming across the Ohio River.

Lin Wang, a Burmese elephant that served with the Chinese Ex-
peditionary Force during the Sino-Japanese War (1937-1945) and
later moved to Taiwan with the Kuomintang army. Lin Wang became a fond childhood memory among many Taiwanese. When
he died in 2003, he was (and still is) the longest-living captive elephant at 86.

Mahmoud, the lead elephant in the army of Abraha, which at-
tacked the Kaaba in Mecca. Thus, the year became known as the
Year of the Elephant and provided a historical ready-reference for
the birth date of the prophet Muhammad of the Muslim religion.

Mamie, an African elephant at the Knoxville Zoo who painted.
She died March 10, 2006 at 45 years old.

Mary a.k.a. "Mighty Mary" and "Murderous Mary", a circus elephant executed on September 13, 1916 in Erwin, Tennessee. She
was hanged by a railroad derrick car at the Clinchfield Railroad
yard. This is the only known elephant hanging in history. Mary,
who toured with the Sparks World Famous Shows circus, killed
her inexperienced keeper, Walter "Red" Eldridge, on September

12, 1916 during a circus parade in Kingsport, Tennessee. Eldridge had supposedly hit Mary's tusk or ear when she wandered from the parade line to eat a piece of discarded watermelon.

Modoc,an Indian Elephant who performed in the North Circus in New York,N.Y., and later starred on Ralph Helfer's famous 1960's show,Daktari. Two books involve her, The Beauty of the Beasts, and Modoc, both by Ralph Helfer.

Mona - euthanized June 21, 2007 at the Birmingham Zoo in Birmingham, Alabama. Thought, at 60, to have been the oldest Asian elephant in the United States. After the death of her companion, Susie, Mona's health and living conditions were the subject of a long campaign to have her transferred out of the zoo to a sanctuary.

Norma Jean, struck by lightning, c. 1972, during a circus parade in Oquawka, Illinois. She was buried where she died, and a marker now lies on this spot.

Old Bet, an early American circus elephant owned by Hachaliah Bailey. On July 24, 1816, she was shot and killed while on tour near Alfred, Maine by a farmer who thought it was sinful for poor people to waste money on a traveling circus. Old Bet's owner responded by building a three story memorial called the Elephant Hotel which now serves as a town hall.

Osama bin Laden, a rogue elephant which killed at least 27 people in India from 2004 to 2006.

Packy (1962—), resident of Oregon Zoo (formerly Washington Park Zoo, originally Portland Zoo) in Portland, Oregon. First Asian elephant born in the Western Hemisphere in 44 years. Now the patriarch of the zoo's herd and has sired seven offspring (although four have died).

Elefante Pino, (12/15/1981-present) Cuba's most famous elephant. Was housed in the Camaguey zoo since in captivity. Pino is best known for it's love affair with a goat that entered its enclosure from a neighboring exhibit.

Queenie (elephant) (—1944), gave rides for children at Melbourne Zoo for 40 years.

Queenie (waterskiing elephant) (1952—2011), noted in the late 1950s and early 1960s for waterskiing for entertainment.

Raja, elephant who carried the holiest Buddhist shrine in Kandy, Sri Lanka

Rita, (1925-1944), elephant best known for its ability to write question marks when presented with canvas and brush.

Renee, Toledo Zoo's master elephant artist; received formal art training in 1995

Rogue elephant of Aberdare Forest, a ferocious bull elephant killed by J. A. Hunter in the Aberdare Range, Kenya

Rosie the Elephant, famous for promoting Miami Beach, Florida

Ruby, (1973–1998), elephant artist, resided at the Phoenix Zoo; at least one painting by her was sold for $100,000

Salt and Sauce, considered the most famous British elephants of their era and mentioned in several circus books

Shanthi at the National Zoo in Washington D.C. plays the harmonica and various horn instruments, ending her songs with a crescendo.

Sissy, an elephant at the El Paso Zoo. In 1999, a videotape showed trainers beating Sissy. After a long public debate, it was determined that Sissy would be sent to an Elephant Sanctuary in Tennessee.

Suleiman the elephant, presented in 1551 to Maximilian II, the Holy Roman Emperor, by John III, the King of Portugal, and named after the Ottoman Sultan, Suleiman the Magnificent

Surapa, Buffalo Zoo's abstract elephant artist

Surus ("the Syrian"), mentioned as the bravest of Hannibal's 37 war elephants which crossed the Alps in 218 BC during the Second Punic War, by Cato the Elder in his book Origines.

Suzi, the only African bush elephant in Pakistan, residing in Lahore Zoo

Tai, known for featuring in the films Larger than Life and Water for Elephants

Tarra, first elephant to retire at the Elephant Sanctuary in Tennessee

Timur, first elephant to be photographed in the wild (May 6, 1896)

Topsy the elephant, circus elephant on Coney Island. She was killed by electrocution after killing three people within three years. Thomas Edison suggested the method of execution and filmed the result.

Tuffi, a young female elephant who fell from Wuppertal's suspended monorail into the river Wupper on July 21, 1950 (and survived the fall)

Toung Taloung, "the Sacred White Elephant of Burma", purchased by P. T. Barnum from the King of Siam for $250,000 – said to be the origin of the expression White Elephant meaning something "more expensive to keep than its worth"

Tusko, billed as the meanest elephant

Tyke, a circus elephant who on August 20, 1994 in Honolulu, Hawaii, killed her trainer Allen Campbell and gored her groom Dallas Beckwith, causing severe injuries during a Circus International performance before hundreds of horrified spectators. Tyke then bolted from the arena and ran through downtown streets of Kakaako for more than 30 minutes. Police fired 86 shots at Tyke, who eventually collapsed from the wounds and died.

Ziggy, a famously rebellious elephant from Brookfield Zoo

6

the! exclamation! mark! is! a truly! incredible! mark. no! other! mark! comes! close! to! its! power! or! affect. if! someone! told! you, in! a world! without! the! exclamaiton! mark! that! there! was! a single! mark! or! pair! of! marks! or! a single! letter! that! affected! the! marks! around! it! to! such! an! extent! and! so! reliably! to! change! meaning! entirely! to! destroy! relationships! or! end! empires! perhaps! though! i don't! know! of! any! specific! examples! of! that! i'm! sure! it! must! have! occurred. the! exclamation! mark! is! such! a powerful! and! individual! mark, rarely! is! it! altered! by! what! is! around! it, instead! it! alters! everything. even! the! question! mark! loses! its! power! to! some! extent. it! can! sometimes, rarely, be (bracketed! in) and! be! confiend! to! irony! that! way! but! in! nearly! every! situation! it! is! dominant
??
??
??

???
???
???
???
???
???
???
???
???
???
?? is
only a single word, or not a word at all

still? something? is? different?

you'll? never? know?

can't? ever? know?

the? weird? thing? is? that? it? seems? to? be? pointing? up-?and?right? as? if? into? the? distant? sky? as? if? questioning? some? being? up? there? a? god? or? someone? on? a? high? hill? or? some? other? vantage? point? where? you? can? see? a? lot?

my mother is going to everest this saturday. she was watching a programme about yeti and the people on it went up everest to try to see if they could find one but they went up way too fast and so they wern't aclimatised and so they started to get big massive headaches which was altitude sickness which means their brains weren't getting enough oxygen. the helicoptor couldn't land because of the weather or something so they basically had to just run down the mountain. seems amazing. what were they running from, really. the air. but terrified.

slowly, very slowly asphyxiating.

she was a little unnerved by this, my mother, but she'll be fine

i have been meaning to write about my mother on facebook for a while. she's quite amazing

you know in human dna, i read, there are sections that are just the dna of centures old viruses that have spliced themselves in for some reason they either don't know or i can't remember. and the dna is just there, not doing anything, like an old file on your hard disk in a folder you've forgotten about. and i want to write like that i guess. like there is a little ancient segment that has worked its way in clean and unmodified and here

cup to Frankie, then returned to his seat on the couch.

"You drink that up now," Orphah told frankie, who sipped it until it cooled off, then gulped it down as fast as he could.

"I'm done," he said, laying the cup on the floor. Marcus immediately picked it p and brought it to the kitchen.

"You're like Marcus here 'fore he got fixed up." Orphah shook her head in gentle remonstrange. "Believin' the faster you do a thing the qicker it's done."

"City ain't country, Aunt Orphah," said Marcus. "You don't act quick sometimes, someone get over on you."

'Where am I?'

'Where everyone is who can't make the ultimate decision, this is the city of Lost Chances, and this, the Room of the Final Disappointment. You see, you can climb as high as you like, but if you've already made the Fundamental Mistake, you end up here, in this room. You can change your role but never your circumstance. It's too late for all that now, toodle-ooo, I'm about to become a buyer.'

'Jeanette,' said Melanie, 'I think you've got a temperature.'

She was sittinb beside me, drinking a cup of tea. She looked tired and crumpled like a balloon full of old air. I touched her cheek but she winced and pulled away.

'What did they do to you?' I asked.

'Nothing, I repented, and they told me I should try and go away for a week. We can't see eachother, it's wrong.' She started to tug at the quilt and I couldn't bear it anymore. I think we cried eachother to sleep, but somewhere in the night I stretched out to her and kissed her and kissed her until we were both sweating and crying with mixed up bodies and swollen faces. She was still asleep when I heard Miss Jewsbury sound her horn.

it is. Just there, maybe forever. Who knows how long the internet will last, you know, who knows. sometimes id ream about what it will be like afterwards. and sometimes i think, i have to save these things because one they they won't be here anymore and we will look back on the internet as something fondly remembered. but then, perhaps people thought the same about...

...there is suddenly no technology that seems permanent.

Dear Novelist, Warrior, Wizard—and Finisher,

Thank you for creating me! I love my main character's conflict. I'm a little scared of my antagonist's menacing behavior, but, hey, that's what antagonists do. And my setting—I can't get enough details. More please!

But I'm worried because I keep hearing tales about writers withering from NaNo's infamous Week Two doldrums. I'm sorry, every novel has abandonment issues, and I want our story to keep going. Please don't leave me when we're just getting started.

If you need to catch up—or if you want to get ahead—let's dive into the day-long NaNoWriMo 2013 Writing Marathon and Donation Day this Saturday, November 9. It's time to shake your fist at writer's block and yell, "I'm writing a novel this month, and I will not be stopped."

Write Until You Drop—and Win Donation Day Prizes

To join in, NaNoWriMo's cast of spectacularly entertaining staff and MLs will be livestreaming throughout the day. Or check your regional forum to see if your Municipal Liaison has something planned.

No matter if you write with others or in your pajamas, join the #NaNoThon on Twitter and donate to win gobsmackingly great hourly prizes (including Kindles, handwritten pep talks from NaNo founder Chris Baty, and a grand prize of a Gotham Writers Workshop class) that will be raffled off throughout the day. Our goal is to raise $50,000 of our overall $1.2 million yearly goal.

Why donate? NaNoWriMo is a nonprofit dedicated to helping everyone tell their story because everyone's story matters. I suggest a donation of $25 to commit to finishing me—an experience you'll remember forever. Also, your donation helps others become super-fantastic creators, including the 100,000 kids and teens who receive free novel writing resources from NaNo's Young Writers Program.

Please help NaNoWriMo run the course for years to come. We need more creators in this world.

With anticipation of the story to come,

Your fist-pumping, fun-loving novel

P.S. If you can't donate, there are more ways to give.

P.P.S. In case I didn't say it well, read others' takes on why it's important to donate to NaNoWriMo.

i so love oranges are not the only fruit. i so love it. i have probably only read two or three books twice, and that is one of them and i don't remember the others. if you're reading this novel and you're reading this now, stop reading it and go and get a copy of oranges are not the only fruit by jeanette winterson and read it.

scarlett said i should run a book tour for my novel. i think it's an excellent idea and i will do it. now taking bookings for... idk, some time in the future. ask my future publisher

Greetings! You contacted me some time ago. In response to your email enclosed you will find more details on available positions and the labor agreement. This current opportunity is available immediately. I hope you will become a member of our team because you match our qualifications and we look forward to working with you.We have new tasks in your area starting now.

Grab a Mystically FAST Spooky Instant Dedicated Server

Grab a Mystically FAST Spooky Instant Dedicated Server

What a potential Fourier was consciously destroyed in this patient described

by the psychiatrist Volnat: "He began to lose all capacity to distinguish

between himself and the external world. Everything that happened in the world

also happened in his body. He could not put a bottle between two shelves in a

cupboard because the shelves might come together and break the bottle. And

that would hurt inside his head, as if his head was wedged between the

shelves. He could not shut a suitcase, because pressing the things in the case

would press inside his head. If he walked into the street after closing all

the doors and windows of his house, he felt uncomfortable, be-

cause his brain
was compressed by the air, and he had to go back home to open a door or a
window. 'For me to be at ease', he said, 'I must have open space .... I must
have the freedom of my space. It's a battle with the things all around me'."

The Consul stopped. He read the inscription: "No se puede vivir sin amar."

Feel like im not alive :((
from New York, NY
IM NOT ALIVE

its feel like im not alive.
i hope im not alive much longer tbh
Reject my follow?okay go ahead
Unfollow me?Have fun
Not reply and pretend Im not alive? keep doing that yea bc thats how you get a girl back
percy real live be walking over me like im not alive
im not alive to do shit i hate day after day, im alive to do shit i wanna do day after day
from Rochester, NH
no, no, not school im not alive rn
"im not alive if im lonely , so please dont leave..."
If Im not alive tomorrow it's because that spider went and got his spider mafia and they killed me while I was sleeping.
SO TIRED. PRETTY SURE IM NOT ALIVE.
IM NOT ALIVE
OH MY GOD! CLAUDIO BIELER! 112TH MINUTE AND IM NOT ALIVE ANYMORE. WE LOVE YOU, WE LOVE YOU, WE LOVE YOU!
Finally home and in bed. Im not alive anymore
IM NOT ALIVE ANYMORE OH FUCK
Im always worried about my future as if im not alive yet, im not alive so stop
IVE GONE FOR TOO LONG LIVING LIKE IM NOT ALIVE

im not alive if im lonely
so please dont leave

Im not alive and Im not dead I just see my goals are impossible
and I get further from them all What a world without you holds I
had to know
i always smell lik e vanilla I Love My Life But Im Not Alive Or
Maybe Its Been A While Since I Died
im not dead, but im not alive.
(please bring me back to life)
im not dead but i have no feeeling im not decayin but i have no
soul im not alive but meerly a walking body
LANA TWEETED AND IT WAS A TEASER FOR TROPICO IM NOT
ALIVE
Idc that deadass hurts my feelings when niggas do that like im
not alive or something like a fucking out cast just using me.
this is not even im not alive giht now holy fukcking shit colton
haynes
Im not alive unless I am creating http://bit.ly/ZKmgMh
Im not alive if im lonely so please dont leave
IVE GONE FOR TOO LONG LIVING LIKE IM NOT ALIVE #VoteP-
ARAMOREonEMA2013 #VOTEPARAMORE x
tao's......happy....trail......... im not alive
Im not alive anymore
Im sorry im not alive to write down when ur fucking girlfriend
came home unless she bought me food. Take a note bro
I've been going on for too long living like im not alive.
agh sana im not alive right now :(((
im not alive right now. ths sucks
Im not alive if im lonely. So please dont leave. Was it something
I said or just my personality.
Cut yourself in conversation, cut a line to make me feel alive.
Cuz you know im not alive.
Im gone for too long living like im not alive..
Im not alive at all , Im just living most of the time .
I feel like im not alive right now...

Sometimes i wish im not alive so that i dont undergo this feeling my coffee maker decided not to work today... aka im not alive yet

Its not easy to hide all this damage inside. I'll carry it with me, until im not alive.

story of my life is gsjdkdbhakdhakdbsk. i died and no im not alive now.. <3 :-* :-* :-*

i love my life but im not alive,
maybe its been a while since i died
Im not alive
Im not alive today.

I hope tht shid happends wen im not alive. IOn give fuggs bout yall.

it's not hard to want to kiss people, it's not hard at all. it's really eas.y. i am so amazed by how easy it is all of the time. there are a few barriers to actually going through with it, sometimes, but it is very easy to want to. does seem like an act of will though. there are people who i find very attractive who i never want to kiss exactly, not in the same way that i do people i do want to kiss.

do you know what i mean? it's somethng different

it's something about agency, maybe

when i am near someone and i want to kiss them i guess it's serious

i have kissed... 1,2,3,4,5,6,7,8,9,10 people

one of them i don't count sometimes because it was really bad but today i am counting them.

You know, if talking to me is about as pleasant as having your wisdom teeth forcibly removed without anaesthetic, then please just say so.

If you're angry, just say so.

You may be strong enough to contact me digitally, but I'm not strong enough to wait to hear what you have to say in different segments.
I'm sorry. I shouldn't have contacted you...I just did.
I'm sorry.

00:32:31 A: cool
      What do you feel like to be desired?
      I mean 'in general' I guess

00:36:30 B: rephrase?

00:37:43 A: Presuming you have felt desired, viscerally rather than theoretically, what did it feel like?

00:40:22 B: mixed.
      varied
      when I was younger it was thrilling I guess, exciting, new.
      And then as it became more real, complex, as I became more sexualised, I guess. It was... imposed upon me I guess. And I hated it. HATED it.
      It made me feel ill, horrible, skin-crawly, worthless
      it made me doubt whether people saw me
      it made me question my value as a person as opposed to an object
      I think that was largely due to having been involved in a less than ideal or healthy relationship when really I was too young for any of it/
00:45:16 A: uhuh

00:45:28 B: Anyway, I got over it
      haha

now...still varies
sometimes I like it, sometimes it's
empowering, but only because I know how
to play with that power
other times itspurely an ego trip and I do it
deliberately, make myself an object to be
desired
other times its surprising
even comforting, reaffirming
sometimes it makes me want to crawl
under a rock and die
usually I guess I dont think much of it, or
Im not entirely sure I beleive it.
I think I only power trip when Im not
REALLY emotionally engaged with
someone
WHen I genuinely care about someone, it's
just something you experience I guess.
Knowing that you're desired...alays all
those stupid paranoias I carry around with
me.

i should email her again soon.
You're too cute: on being an anon and the escape from mascu-
linity
when I see photos of beautiful women I sometimes cry. such an
intense conflict is built in me at that moment, I can't contain it.
is that patriarchal? I don't know, I feel like maybe it is. I don't tell
anyone.
I joined okcupid but I never message anyone. I joined so that I
could find beautiful intriguing people and never message them.
being a man has become untenable for me. my desire feels like
guilt.
I saw a profile today. tall, six foot, bisexual, short blonde hair,
parted the same way as mine. Speaks french, identifies as a poet
'oh yeah i don't usually use caps i hope that doesn't get on your
nerves'

on okcupid I decided never to use caps, I don't know why.
she is taller than me. I so, so much desire women who are taller than me. only an inch but
one of her favourite books is I am like October when I am dead by Steve Roggenbuck
"if you call me, i wont answer
i am sitting under the moon inside of a wheelbarrow"
she is taller than me. I think about kissing her for a second but then I stop myself.
feel like that is wrong or bad
feel like that is wrong or bad
I click 'Send her a message'
I write 'i just read 'i am like october when i am dead' by steve roggenbuck. i knew of him but i hadn't read that. i really liked it.'
(I am doing these things as I type)
sometimes on tumblr when I see people I feel like I really attracted to I will message them anonymously. even really simple things about liking their tumblr. not always that, sometimes it is sexual. not too much, just a little, sometimes gradually. it is fun to do. I can only do this anonymously. there are two reasons
the first is that I feel uncomfortable with my desire
I have just been messaged on okcupid, as I write this. it says: 'Hey I can't tell if you're terrifying or attractive, js.'
what does js mean? is it a sign-off? or something else?
as I was saying:
the first is that I feel uncomfortable with my desire as it comes from a man. Foucault once wrote that the goal of the critique of power is to, I'm paraphrasing, but 'tie it in knots', make all of its actions impossible, take away its agency. I feel like I am the vanguard of men and that feminism is doing this to me. I allow it, I don't resent it. I'm not sure, but I suspect to be a man is becoming unworkable. the only alternative is to become something else.
the second is that by being anon I can fictionalize away all of the sexual dysfunction that comes for me with having a male body and with what 'sex' is
I think, I never want to have sex again. I want something else, something with desire, something with pleasure and bliss, and

the body, and words, and interplay. is sex patriarchal? I suspect it might be, it is hard to me to imagine what is normally called sex being anything other than patriarchal. at the very least, if we were thinking about it, sex really is too ruined by patriarchy to do anything other than scrap it and start again with something new. Baudrillard called his solution seduction, but I can't trust Baudrillard anymore, after all he's said.

my body, personally, resists sex. I am embarrassed. I don't know if it is common amongst anxious men like me. in relationships, I start off unable to 'last' more than a minute or two, and end up not being able to orgasm at all. the transition is very smooth, such that there is a space of maybe a month in which I last a socially acceptable amount of time.

I never have piv sex, though, I can't do it. it upsets me a lot. it's very exciting as an act, but it really upsets me.

I have worked out recently that if I hold someone very very tightly for maybe 3 minutes after my climax I can stave off most of the intense feeling of sadness and emptiness that follows orgasm for me.

so I want something new. I have, until now, mostly practiced oral sex, but truly anything seen as 'confined to' is not enough. there has to be something new. it exists on the edges of my awareness, something spatial, something about occasion, performance, power, place, configuration, apartness, rhythm, tease, language, conversation, interplay. I cannot as yet describe any particular acts or movements, but I think I will have to start with my hands and continue along those lines.

(I once was involved with a girl who felt quite strongly about her faith, and who wouldn't have sex before marriage. I loved this girl, an awful lot. I thought about marrying her, though we both knew it would never happen, it was nice to think about though

we would kiss a lot, she was a ferocious and amazing kisser, the best I've ever had. it was so, so good. but it would get to a certain point, a certain moment or level or intensity and she would pull back and we would stare at eachother for a few minutes, and then she might apologise and I might say, no, it's fine, I don't mind. I think she was used to men being annoyed at having led them on or something. but I loved it, because for me I think kissing is the final sexual frontier at which I feel safe and happy.

two things happened with her, which were then and now remain two of the most sexually exciting things that have ever, ever happened to me:

1. once we were kissing and I had put my hand up the back of her jumper to touch her back and her shoulder. one incredible, unforgettable moment followed. she grabbed my arm and moved it down around her torso and pushed my hand onto her breast

I was mostly unprepared for this, and I was very unsure as to how to proceed considering I thought this was already beyond her comfort zone and I was quite sure any further would be way too far. after maybe 30 seconds she pushed my hand away and we stared at eachother for a few minutes

2. she was kissing my chest, and my sternum, and then down my stomach. she stopped somewhere above my navel, and looked up at me for a moments. then, as she moved back up to kiss my mouth, I felt her hand run across me, base to tip, and I was hard. she was distracting me with her gaze, and it was almost like she didn't mean to do it, or that she wanted me to think that or even not to notice at all. but it was such an intentional movement that I feel now like it must have been deliberate. she wanted to feel me.

those two things, without being sex, remain alight in my mind as two of the most intensely exciting things that another person has ever done to me.

and I want more of that, I think in that is the sort of sex I want, something so weighty and intense and full of desire and honesty, that transcend the patriarchal sexual script. that doesn't involve turn taking, or me climaxing last because I lose interest straight after orgasm, that is fraught with exciting powerplay and a sharp novelty and danger

am I a good terrifying or a bad terrifying? I want to be a good terrifying. I want to be a cliff-edge terrifying and not a he's-looking-at-me terrifying. I'm not sure if I can be. I'm not sure if that is open to me within patriarchy.

I look at women and cry because of this. because I was born into this body and this cultural position that precludes me from relat-

ing to women without patriarchy being present. some are optimis-
tic and say that we can counteract this with awareness but I don't
think I agree. I hope somehow that I can counteract it by under-
mining my privilege and encouraging women to take power over
me.

I don't know if that will help. maybe it will help me, I don't know
today i have heartburn and a longg time ago i called it badfeeling, because i used to get it all of the time, whole afternoons i don't
know why and i used to call it badfeeling because i thought it was
just emotional. it makes me very upset and resltess and unable to
do anything or focus my mind on anything. but i thought it was interesting because it is a physical sensation that i misinterpreted as
an emotional response. and maybe this is the case always. but also,
this time, perhaps i am misinterpreting an emotional sensation as
a physical one/ it's really hard to tell which is really weird if you
thibk about it. all emotions are physical sensationsbut some are
aboiut things that are 'really there' and some aren't. but... before
we cutpeople up a lot do you think we even had that distinction, do
you think maybe heartburn was an emotional sensation, because
we have no way without looking inside to know where the sensation originates......................................

religious experiences i have had:
  singing hymns in school, i guess. it was a christian school, an-
glican, and there were two main headmasters. the first was a patriarch really. he was a nice man, as far as i remember, but he was
fatherly and paternal and i am not... entirely sure whether it was
a positive thing. he left the post to go back to teaching and he was
my teacher in year five i think. he had a reputation for being very
shouty and strict, and my mother said in the run up to my being
taught by him — he will sort you out — but not in a menacing way,
i guess she just thought a lot of him as a teacher and the idea was
that he would sort out all the things that were wrong with my per-
sonality/learning as a child. namely my writing and english skills,
which i guess is ironic considering i am soon to be a novelist. the
second headteacher was far more overtly religious than him, and
one assembly i remember particularly aas it is in hindsight rather
sinister. she said something like, you have the choice as to whether or not to believe in noah and the flood, but science says there

was a flood 40 million years ago, you can't argue with that, that's what science says. she is dead from cancer now, i believe.

IN THE MIDST OF THAT GLOOM COMES ENOCH – A MAN WHOM THE SCRIPTURE RECORDS HAD "WALKED" WITH GOD. OH BEHOLD THE GLORY OF A MAN ONCE AGAIN RESTORED TO THE PRE-SIN STATE OF BEING ABLE TO WALK WITH GOD. BEFORE ADAM SINNED, HE WALKED WITH GOD. HE FELLOW-SHIPPED WITH GOD. HE CONVERSED WITH GOD. GOD MUST HAVE SHARED HIS HEART WITH HIM, FOR MAN WAS MADE FOR FELLOWSHIP WITH GOD. AND THEN CAME THE SERPENT AND THE SIN IN ADAM – WHERE ADAM HID HIMSELF FROM GOD AND STOPPED THE FELLOWSHIP.

rememberence day parade, to the church. there were hymns. i think rememberence day is a bit of a shame, as in, the way it's taught. because the world wars, the second world war particularly i think, is one of the most interesting and tragic moments of euro-pean history, and there is an awful lot to remember, an awful lot to say 'never again' to, but the line always seems to be 'those who gave their lives for us' which is such a bullshit line, really, and... i remember, as a child and adolescent, thinking, what the heck am i supposed to be remembering here? the condition of the trenches? some abstract soldier and what he might have had to experience?

THANK YOU JESUS FOR A GOOD WEEK. I CONTINUE TO PRAISE YOU FOR ALL THE GRACE YOU HAVE GIVEN TO ME. IN-DEED YOU HAVE WALK ME OUT OF THE VALLEY OF TROUBLE. I LOVE YOU JESUS. NOW I GET TO UNDERSTAND GOD'S TIMING, I WON'T BE SO STRESSED OUT. I HAVE LEARN TO UNDERSTAND YOUR TIMING SO THAT EVERYTHING IS IN CONTROL BASED ON YOUR APPOINTED TIMING. WHATEVER I DESIRE, I KNOW YOU WILL MAKE IT HAPPEN. I CONTINUE TO PRAY THAT I CAN TRUST GOD I DON'T HAVE TO STRUGGLE. JESUS I CONTINUE TO PRAY FOR FAVOUR AND WISDOM FOR MY CHILDREN. MAY THEY CONTINUE TO ENJOY THE MILK AND HONEY THAT FLOW THROUGH YOU TO THEM. I KNOW THEIR FUTURE IS BRIGHT. I HAVE BREAK THE CURSE THAT HAS HAPPENED. MY FUTURE GENERATION WILL BE SO MUCH MORE BLESS IN TERMS OF FI-NANCE AND GOOD THINGS IN LIFE. I KNOW MY JESUS WILL

LOOK AFTER THEM SO THAT THEY WILL BE BLESSED TO BE A BLESSING. YES JESUS I CONTINUE TO PLACE MY WORK UNDER GRACE AND THAT WHATEVER DIRECTION YOU LEAD ME,I WILL FOLLOW YOU. THANK YOU JESUS FOR THE CONTINUOUS SUPPORT AND LIFTING OF MY LIFE. WITHOUT YOU, I CAN'T IMAGINE MY LIFE. BUT TODAY I CLAIM MY LIFE IS GREAT BECAUSE OF YOU. IN JESUS NAME I PRAY AMEN

my first girlfriend, who has recently had a kid, was a christian from a christian family. she used to go to something called 'the mix', and once i went with her and it was one of the most stressful experiences of my life to date at that time. i didn't really have any understanding of 'anxiety' as a condition as opposed to an emotion at that point, which made it doubly hard in fact. she was there with a few friends who were, transparently, 'christian boys' (i have become able to spot christians, generally, with a few notable false positives...), very nice, clean cut, not overtly threatening but giving the impression of being very well adjusted people. there was a band and people put their hands up like they do,you know, reaching, for jesus or something i guess. there was a point in it in which they asked, quite dramatically, if there was anyone who wanted to come up and be saved, maybe people who didn't think of themselves as christian necessarily or people who had fallen off somehow. a few people went up, i knew that they were talking about me, that i could be one of th people going up and i felt a pressure, being wth this girl, that it would be positive for her and my relationship to go up there. i didn't go up there, but the pressure, like being stuck between two closing walls, was very strong and i felt very uncomfortable.

I HEARD THIS STORY ON THE RADIO RECENTLY: A WOMAN WAS MOURNING AND GRIEVING OVER SINS SHE COMMITTED AFTER BECOMING A BELIEVER AND FOLLOWER OF JESUS. SHE HAD CONFESSED THEM TO GOD BUT WAS STRUGGLING WITH THE FACT THAT EVEN AFTER KNOWING JESUS AND RECEIVING THE MERCY OF GOD - SHE STILL SINS...AND EVEN WANTS TO SOMETIMES. SHE WAS TALKING WITH HER PASTOR ABOUT THIS AND HE ASKED HER: "DURING YOUR ENTIRE LIFETIME, BEFORE AND AFTER YOUR SALVATION, HOW MANY SINS DID

YOU COMMIT AFTER JESUS DIED AND ROSE AGAIN?" SHE AN-
SWERED, "ALL OF THEM." HE ASSURED HER, "JESUS DIED FOR
ALL OF OUR SINS. YOU CONFESS, HE FORGIVES. THEN YOU
MUST RECEIVE HIS FORGIVENESS BY FAITH, JUST LIKE YOU RE-
CEIVED YOUR SALVATION BY FAITH. ASK HIM DAILY FOR THE
STRENGTH TO LIVE ACCORDING TO HIS WAY AND HE WILL
GIVE IT. REMEMBER THAT THE BOOK OF 1 JOHN WAS WRITTEN
TO BELIEVERS. AND 1 JOHN 1:9 SAYS, "IF WE CONFESS OUR SINS,
HE IS FAITHFUL AND JUST TO FORGIVE US AND CLEANSE US
FROM ALL UNRIGHTEOUSNESS." SO, KEEP CONFESSING AND
RECEIVING HIS MERCY AND EVERY DAY, WALK HUMBLY WITH
YOUR GOD." AND A FEW DAYS AFTER THAT RADIO BROADCAST
I READ THIS IN SPURGEON'S MORNING AND EVENING: "LOOK
TO THY PERFECT LORD AND REMEMBER THOU ART COMPLETE
IN HIM; THOU ART IN GOD'S SIGHT AS PERFECT AS THOU
HADST NEVER SINNED; NAY MORE THAN THAT, THE LORD OUR
RIGHTEOUSNESS HATH PUT A DIVINE GARMENT ON THEE, SO
THAT THOU HAST MORE THAN THE RIGHTEOUSNESS OF MAN -
THOU HAST THE RIGHTEOUSNESS OF GOD. REMEMBER - NONE
OF THY SINS CONDEMN THEE

my great uncle's funeral. he was cremated. it was the first time
i wore a tie except for at school. my grandmother cried and so did
his wife, they cried together even though they were related only by
marriage and i still find that very touching, since my grandmother, i guess, i have not experienced her as an emotional persn very
much. there was a wake, and i spilt something red on me and i had
to go into the kitchen and someone washed it off of me which i
found very, very embarrassing, even shameful, because this was
the first time, wearing a tie, i felt like i was being treated as an
adult, as a man, and i had failed at this, and it felt like a significant,
betrayal, of my father, maybe

GOD IS GOD AND HE IS OMNISCIENT, OMNIPRESENT AND
OMNIPOTENT AND THAT IS WHY HE IS SOVEREIGN. PEOPLE
ARE MYOPIC, SELFISH AND SELF-SERVING. GOD IS LOVE AND
RESPONDS WITH THE BEST INTEREST OF THE PERSON AND
HIS/HER LOVED ONES IN MIND. DOES THIS TAKE THE STING
OUT OF DEATH? NO!!! GRIEF IS A NATURAL RESPONSE TO LOS-

ING A LOVED ONE IN DEATH. IN ECCLESIASTES 3:1-8 WE FIND THE "THE MYSTERY OF TIME": 1 THERE IS AN OCCASION FOR EVERYTHING, AND A TIME FOR EVERY ACTIVITY UNDER HEAVEN: 2 A TIME TO GIVE BIRTH AND A TIME TO DIE; A TIME TO PLANT AND A TIME TO UPROOT;[1]3 A TIME TO KILL AND A TIME TO HEAL; A TIME TO TEAR DOWN AND A TIME TO BUILD; 4 A TIME TO WEEP AND A TIME TO LAUGH; A TIME TO MOURN AND A TIME TO DANCE; 5 A TIME TO THROW STONES AND A TIME TO GATHER STONES;[2]A TIME TO EMBRACE AND A TIME TO AVOID EMBRACING; 6 A TIME TO SEARCH AND A TIME TO COUNT AS LOST; A TIME TO KEEP AND A TIME TO THROW AWAY; 7 A TIME TO TEAR AND A TIME TO SEW; A TIME TO BE SILENT AND A TIME TO SPEAK; 8 A TIME TO LOVE AND A TIME TO HATE; A TIME FOR WAR AND A TIME FOR PEACE. WE NEED TO KEEP IN MIND THAT DEATH IS THE RESULT OF SIN. WHEN MAN SINNED, DEATH AND DECAY ENTERED INTO THE WORLD. GOD INTENDED FOR MANKIND TO LIVE IN A PERPETUAL GARDEN OF EDEN. BECAUSE MAN SINNED, DEATH ENTERED THE WORLD. HE KNEW THAT THE CONSEQUENCES OF SIN WOULD BE ETERNAL DEATH FOR MANKIND. GOD HAD A PLAN BEFORE HE CREATED THE WORLD TO REDEEM MANKIND FROM ETERNAL DEATH. GOD ALLOWED HIS ONLY SON, JESUS TO LEAVE HEAVEN AND COME TO EARTH, BE BORN, LIVE AS A HUMAN AND GIVE HIS LIFE THROUGH THE SHEDDING OF HIS BLOOD TO REDEEM ALL WHO WOULD BELIEVE ON HIM. JESUS HAD THE FREEDOM TO CHOOSE TO SIN OR TO REMAIN SINLESS. HE WAS TEMPTED IN ALL WAYS AS HUMANS. HE REMAINED SINLESS AND THUS WAS THE PERFECT SACRIFICE TO PAY FOR THE SINS OF MANKIND. HIS SHED BLOOD PAID FOR AND BROKE THE SIN BARRIER BETWEEN MAN AND GOD. ALL ANY PERSON HAS TO DO IS BELIEVE THAT HE GAVE HIS LIFE FOR HIM/HER - ASK HIM FOR FORGIVENESS AND TO COME INTO HIS/HER LIFE. WHEN A PERSON DOES THAT HE/SHE IS BORN INTO GOD'S FAMILY FOREVER. THIS IS THE MIRACLE OF BEING BORN-AGAIN. IT IS DIFFICULT FOR MOST OF US TO SEE THE VALUE IN TRAGEDY - ONLY GOD FROM HIS VANTAGE POINT KNOWS THE END RESULT OF A TRAGEDY.

a girl who for a time was one of the most important people in my life was what i would term strongly religious, maybe 'devout' is a good term. we got on very well, and i would say we were very fond of eachother, very compatible. she is, i suppose, the only person i have spent more than a day or two around without getting anxious and uncomfortable. all except that one of her most important ambitions was marriage, and marriage within her faith. after a time she decided to go away on a mission, to russia, and before she did she phoned me up and cried and told me she loved me, and i said i loved her, and maybe that is the last time i ever said that, to anyone. she is getting married soon, i think.

AFTER JESUS SHOWERED ALL OF THIS LOVE AND HONOR ON JUDAS ONE WOULD THINK THAT JUDAS WOULD CHANGE HIS MIND. THE DEVIL HAD PROMPTED JUDAS TO BETRAY JESUS BUT TO THIS POINT HE HAD DONE NOTHING ABOUT IT. I WOULD GUESS, THEORETICALLY, JUDAS COULD HAVE SAID "NO" TO SATAN'S PROMPTING. JUDAS, HOWEVER, DID NOT SAY "NO". JESUS SAID WHEN ASKED WHO WOULD BETRAY HIM, "IT IS THE ONE TO WHOM I WILL GIVE THIS PIECE OF BREAD WHEN I HAVE DIPPED IT IN THE DISH." THEN JESUS DIPPED THE BREAD AND JUDAS ACCEPTED IT. JESUS KNEW JUDAS WOULD BETRAY HIM YET HE SHOWERED HIS LOVE ON HIM. JUDAS COULD HAVE BACKED OUT BUT HE DIDN'T. CAN YOU IMAGINE THIS? ONE OF MY BIGGEST FEARS AND A BIG FEAR FOR MANY IS UNREQUITED LOVE. LOVE ISN'T MUCH FUN UNLESS IT'S MUTUAL. UNREQUITED LOVE IS THE THEME OF MANY GREAT WORKS IN THE GENRE OF TRAGEDY. JESUS LOVED JUDAS EVEN THOUGH JUDAS DECIDED NOT TO LOVE HIM BACK. MANY WONDER, "HOW COULD JUDAS DO THAT?" HERE'S THE TRUTH: JUDAS IS ONE OF MILLIONS. JESUS HAS SHOWN US ALL "THE FULL EXTENT OF HIS LOVE" AT THE CROSS. WE HAVE A MORE PERFECT VISION OF THIS LOVE THAN JUDAS DID. HERE'S THE MILLION DOLLAR QUESTION: "HOW COULD WE NOT LOVE JESUS?" YET MILLIONS WILL REJECT HIM. JESUS KNEW THAT WHEN HE SACRIFICED HIMSELF ON THE CROSS. IF THAT ISN'T LOVE, I DON'T WHAT IS. LOVE THE ONE WHO LOVED YOU FIRST TODAY.

i find it so amazing that you can take a rubber duck or something and drop it from a plane (i suppose) in the middle of the pacific ocean. what happens to such a duck, i don't know. will it ever find land again? i don't know. how long will it take?

Futures studies (also called futurology and futurism) is the study of postulating possible, probable, and preferable futures and the worldviews and myths that underlie them. There is a debate as to whether this discipline is an art or science. In general, it can be considered as a branch of the social sciences and parallel to the field of history. In the same way that history studies the past, futures studies considers the future. Futures studies (colloquially called "futures" by many of the field's practitioners) seeks to understand what is likely to continue and what could plausibly change. Part of the discipline thus seeks a systematic and pattern-based understanding of past and present, and to determine the likelihood of future events and trends. Unlike the physical sciences where a narrower, more specified system is studied, futures studies concerns a much bigger and more complex world system. The methodology and knowledge are much less proven as compared to natural science or even social science like sociology, economics, and political science.

Three factors usually distinguish futures studies from the research conducted by other disciplines (although all of these disciplines overlap, to differing degrees). First, futures studies often examines not only possible but also probable, preferable, and "wild card" futures. Second, futures studies typically attempts to gain a holistic or systemic view based on insights from a range of different disciplines. Third, futures studies challenges and unpacks the assumptions behind dominant and contending views of the future. The future thus is not empty but fraught with hidden assumptions. For example, many people expect the collapse of the Earth's ecosystem in the near future, while others believe the current ecosystem will survive indefinitely. A foresight approach would seek to analyse and so highlight the assumptions underpinning such views.

Some aspects of the future, such as celestial mechanics, are highly predictable, and may even be described by relatively simple mathematical models. At present however, science has yielded only a special minority of such "easy to predict" physical processes. Theories such as chaos theory, nonlinear science and standard evolutionary theory have allowed us to understand many complex systems as contingent (sensitively dependent on complex environmental conditions) and stochastic (random within constraints), making the vast majority of future events unpredictable, in any specific case.

Not surprisingly, the tension between predictability and unpredictability is a source of controversy and conflict among futures studies scholars and practitioners. Some argue that the future is essentially unpredictable, and that "the best way to predict the future is to create it." Others believe, as Flechtheim, that advances in science, probability, modeling and statistics will allow us to continue to improve our understanding of probable futures, while this area presently remains less well developed than methods for exploring possible and preferable futures.

As an example, consider the process of electing the president of the United States. At one level we observe that any U.S. citizen over 35 may run for president, so this process may appear too unconstrained for useful prediction. Yet further investigation demonstrates that only certain public individuals (current and former presidents and vice presidents, senators, state governors, popular military commanders, mayors of very large cities, etc.) receive the appropriate "social credentials" that are historical prerequisites for election. Thus with a minimum of effort at formulating the problem for statistical prediction, a much reduced pool of candidates can be described, improving our probabilistic foresight. Applying further statistical intelligence to this problem, we can observe that in certain election prediction markets such as the Iowa Electronic Markets, reliable forecasts have been generated over long spans of time and conditions, with results superior to individual experts or polls. Such markets, which may be operated publicly or as an internal market, are just one of several promising frontiers in predictive futures research.

Futures studies is often summarized as being concerned with "three Ps and a W", or possible, probable, and preferable futures, plus wildcards, which are low probability but high impact events (positive or negative), should they occur. Many futurists, however, do not use the wild card approach. Rather, they use a methodology called Emerging Issues Analysis. It searches for the seeds of change, issues that are likely to move from unknown to the known, from low impact to high impact.

n futures research "weak signals" may be understood as advanced, noisy and socially situated indicators of change in trends and systems that constitute raw informational material for enabling anticipatory action. There is confusion about the definition of weak signal by various researchers and consultants. Sometimes it is referred as future oriented information, sometimes more like emerging issues. Elina Hiltunen (2007), in her new concept the future sign has tried to clarify the confusion about the weak signal definitions, by combining signal, issue and interpretation to the future sign, which more holistically describes the change.

"Wild cards" refer to low-probability and high-impact events, such as existential risks. This concept may be embedded in standard foresight projects and introduced into anticipatory decision-making activity in order to increase the ability of social groups adapt to surprises arising in turbulent business environments. Such sudden and unique incidents might constitute turning points in the evolution of a certain trend or system. Wild cards may or may not be announced by weak signals, which are incomplete and fragmented data from which relevant foresight information might be inferred. Sometimes, mistakenly, wild cards and weak signals are considered as synonyms, which they are not.

1. We are in the midst of a historical transformation. Current times are not just part of normal history.
2. Multiple perspectives are at heart of futures studies, including unconventional thinking, internal critique, and cross-cultural comparison.
3. Consideration of alternatives. Futurists do not see themselves as value-free forecasters, but instead aware of multiple possibilities.
4. Participatory futures. Futurists generally see their role as liberating the future in each person, and creating enhanced public ownership of the future. This is true worldwide.[clarification needed]
5. Long term policy transformation. While some are more policy-oriented than others, almost all believe that the work of futurism is to shape public policy, so it consciously and explicitly takes into account the long term.
6. Part of the process of creating alternative futures and of influencing public (corporate, or international) policy is internal transformation. At international meetings, structural and individual factors are considered equally important.
7. Complexity. Futurists believe that a simple one-dimensional or single-discipline orientation is not satisfactory. Trans-disciplinary approaches that take complexity seriously are necessary. Systems thinking, particularly in its evolutionary dimension, is also crucial.

8. Futurists are motivated by change. They are not content merely to describe or forecast. They desire an active role in world transformation.
9. They are hopeful for a better future as a "strange attractor".
10. Most believe they are pragmatists in this world, even as they imagine and work for another. Futurists have a long term perspective.
11. Sustainable futures, understood as making decisions that do not reduce future options, that include policies on nature, gender and other accepted paradigms. This applies to corporate futurists and the NGO. Environmental sustainability is reconciled with the technological, spiritual and post-structural ideals. Sustainability is not a "back to nature" ideal, but rather inclusive of technology and culture.

Many people regard the attainment of the highest possible level of happiness as the most important aspect and primary goal of their lives. Humans have been found in studies to achieve a "baseline happiness," sometimes called the hedonic treadmill, a pre-determined happiness setpoint that a person will return to throughout their lives no matter what happens to him or her, regardless of income, and regardless of the occurrence of events that most people theorize would make a person permanently happy or permanently sad, such as a lottery win or the death of a close relative.

An important discovery that boosts the case for the potential to abolish suffering is the example of deep brain stimulation of the brain's pleasure centers. The direct electrical stimulation does not create tolerance proving that there is a potential to overcome the brain's anhedonic homeostatic mechanisms.[citation needed] Pacemaker-type neurostimulators have been shown to reliably increase observed happiness without causing detriments to functionality: these interventions have proven to actually increase various cognitive and social aspects of human functionality.[citation needed]

Moore v. Regents of the University of California (51 Cal. 3d 120; 271 Cal. Rptr. 146; 793 P.2d 479) was a landmark Supreme Court of California decision filed on July 9, 1990 which dealt with the issue of property rights in one's own body parts. John Moore underwent treatment for hairy cell leukemia at the UCLA Medical Center under the supervision of Dr. David W. Golde. Moore's cancer was later developed into a cell line that was commercialized. The California Supreme Court ruled that Moore had no right to any share of the profits realized from the commercialization of anything developed from his discarded body parts.

The opinion first looked at Moore's claim of property interests under existing law. The court first rejected the argument that a person has an absolute right to the unique products of their body because his products were not unique. "[The cells are] no more unique to Moore than the number of vertebrae in the spine or the chemical formula of hemoglobin." The court then rejected the argument that his spleen should be protected as property in order to protect Moore's privacy and dignity. The court held these interests were already protected by informed consent. The court noted laws that required the destruction of human organs as some indication that the legislature had intended to prevent patients from possessing their extracted organs. Finally, the property at issue may not have been Moore's cells but the cell line created from Moore's cells.

Justice Arabian wrote a concurring opinion stating that the deep philosophical, moral and religious issues that are presented by this case could not be decided by the court.

Justice Broussard concurred in part and dissented in part.

Sham surgery (also called placebo surgery) is a faked surgical intervention that omits the step thought to be therapeutically necessary.

In clinical trials of surgical interventions, sham surgery is an important scientific control. This is because it isolates the specific effects of the treatment as opposed to the incidental effects caused by anesthesia, the incisional trauma, pre- and postoperative care, and the patient's perception of having had a regular operation. Thus sham surgery serves an analogous purpose to placebo drugs, neutralizing biases such as the placebo effect.

In the final test of the series, the Fleetwood-based trawler Carella, with a crew of eighteen, ignored warnings to steer clear and unwittingly sailed through a cloud of plague bacteria (Yersinia pestis) on its return from a fishing trip to the waters around Iceland, causing concern about a possible plague outbreak around its home port in north-west England. The Carella was not stopped for disinfection or medical examination but was kept under covert observation by a destroyer and a fisheries vessel for twenty-one days, and the ship's radio communications were monitored for any kind of medical distress call. The surveillance period included a period of shore-leave at Blackpool, during which the crew mixed with the people of the town as usual. None of the crew became ill.

The incident was dealt with at the highest levels of government, going through the First Sea Lord to the Chancellor of the Exchequer Rab Butler, who was deputising for the absent Winston Churchill. The event was successfully covered up and, after the danger had passed, most of the documents relevant to the case were ordered to be burnt. Even the crew of the Carella were unaware of the incident until approached by a BBC documentary crew more than fifty years later.

i find it so amazing that you can take a rubber duck or something and drop it from a plane (i suppose) in the middle of the pacific ocean. what happens to such a duck, i don't know. will it ever find land again? i don't know. how long will it take?

10

The weather in the morning of the accident flight, as forecast, consisted of an area of heavy precipitation over and to the north and west of Cheyenne, with better conditions to the east, where the flight was headed. As the group were about to board their aircraft, the program director who had taken them to their hotel the previous evening interviewed Dubroff by telephone. Since it began to rain at the airport and the weather seemed to be deteriorating, the director invited her to stay in Cheyenne, but Dubroff's father declined, explaining that they wanted to "beat the storm" which was approaching.

After a telephone discussion with a Casper weather briefer, Reid decided to take off despite the worsening conditions at the airport, and to try to escape the poor weather by turning immediately eastward. Although he was instrument rated, Reid was not instrument current and could not legally operate under instrument flight rules. He decided to file a visual flight rules (VFR) flight plan, and depart under VFR, to be better able to cope with the heavy weather

in his immediate takeoff path and the vicinity of the airport.
As the aircraft began taxiing to the departure runway, it was raining and visibility at the airport fell below the three mile minimum required for VFR flight. Cheyenne's control tower advised the Cessna about the reduced visibility and that the "field is IFR." Reid then requested and received from the control tower a special VFR clearance to allow him to exit the airport's control zone visually, despite the reduced visibility.

in my first year of university i heard word that two boys who i knew, vaguely, from my secondary school, a few years younger than me, had died in a light aircraft crash. it's upsetting and terrifying how frequently death happens. i imagine it like being in the blitz. maybe the bombs are far away or near to you, or both, right now, but you know that eventually they will be very close and you have no way of knowing who is making porridge 100' below a bomb right now

but someone is

Accident summary

Date	Thursday, April 11, 1996
	8:24 AM MST
Summary	Deliberate take off because of media
	commitments
	Foul weather
	Pilot error
Site	Cheyenne, Wyoming, United States
Passengers	1
Crew	2
Fatalities	3 (all)
Aircraft type	Cessna 177B
Aircraft name	Cardinal
Operator	Joe Reid
Registration	N35207 C/n
	msn:17702266
Flight origin	Half Moon Bay Airport
	Half Moon Bay, California, United States

1st stopover	Elko Regional Airport
	Elko, Nevada
2nd stopover	Rock Springs – Sweetwater County Airport
	Rock Springs, Wyoming
Last stopover	Cheyenne Regional Airport
	Cheyenne, Wyoming
Destination	Lincoln Airport
	Lincoln, Nebraska

At 8:24 AM MST, Dubroff's aircraft began its takeoff roll from Cheyenne's runway 30 to the northwest, in rain, strong gusty crosswinds and turbulence. According to witnesses, the plane lifted off and climbed slowly, with its nose high and its wings wobbling. It began a gradual right turn, and after reaching an altitude of a few hundred feet, the plane rolled out of its turn, then descended rapidly, crashing at a near-vertical angle into a street in a residential neighborhood. Dubroff, her father, and Reid were all killed by trauma sustained from impact forces. Reid, who was legally the pilot in command for all of Dubroff's flights, was apparently manipulating the controls during this particular flight segment.

what is it about air crashes that terrify us so much more than car crashes. i suppose maybe when you are in a plane you might have a lot of time to think about crashing when you are crashing, and you can do nothing about it. i don't know how long it takes for a plane to go from being up in the air to crashing into the ground, but maybe what would surprise you the most if you were in one is how long it takes. it might take seven minutes. how long is seven minutes when you're waiting to have a tooth out or take a test. it's a long time. how long is seven minutes when you're going to crash in an airplane into the ground and probably die and probably not very well. you know not everyone gets into the brace position, i mean, i suppose, in seven minutes you might decide you don't want to

Like most flight instructors giving dual instruction, Reid was seated on the right side, while the aircraft's primary flight instruments were mounted on the left, in front of Dubroff in this case.

Investigators speculated that because of the heavy rain in his immediate climb path, Reid's forward visibility became greatly restricted. So to maintain control through the climbing right turn, he would have had to turn his head to the left to see the flight instruments (most critically the attitude and airspeed indicators) and to the right to see the ground through the side window. Such side-to-side head motion, combined with the worsening flight visibility during the climb and the reduced stall margin, could have led to spatial disorientation and loss of control.

Ted Koppel said the media's "ravenous attention" contributed to the tragedy.

After the crash, there were claims that the media frenzy around the "bogus" record attempt contributed to the accident by helping promote the flight and pressuring its schedule. This was supported by the NTSB, which determined that the pressure induced by the intense media attention was a "contributing factor" in the accident. ABC's Ted Koppel reflected on the media's role in the tragedy on Nightline: "We need to begin by acknowledging our own contribution...We feed one another: those of you looking for publicity and those of us looking for stories." Koppel ended by asking "whether we in the media...by our ravenous attention contribute to this phenomenon," and answered: "We did."

"We did, we did."

Lloyd Dubroff, Jessica's father, was Lisa Blair Hathaway's common-law husband when Jessica and her brother were born. In 1990 he separated from Hathaway, and in 1991 he married Melinda Anne Hurst, with whom he had a child in 1992. In December 1992, Hathaway gave birth to Jessica's full sister.

Before his death in the crash, Lloyd Dubroff bought four separate life insurance policies, each for US$750,000. Two of the policies named Hathaway as beneficiary and two named Melinda Dubroff, so that each was to receive $1.5 million in the event of his death. After the crash, Melinda Dubroff sued Hathaway for Hathaway's $1.5 million: Melinda Dubroff's attorney Roy Litherland said in a San Mateo County court that the $1.5 million Hathaway was designated was "in excess of any reasonable level of child support." In December 1996, Lisa Hathaway filed a counter-suit against Melinda Dubroff and Lloyd Dubroff's estate for $1.5 million, the exact amount of money Lloyd Dubroff intended, saying Lloyd Dubroff "gave his word he would care for and support [her] for the rest and remainder of her natural life."

On December 18, 1997, San Mateo County Superior Court Judge Judith Kozloski ruled that the insurance benefits should be split equally between the two women, $1.5 million each, and dismissed the other claims.

when i die who will get my spices. will they be thrown away? they're quite particular. i chose them quite particular. but i suppose, no one will cook like i did anymore, and no one will know what to do with them. asafoedita, where does it fit? where does it go? will they know that they can't add it right at the beginning like you'd think? and the cinnammon, what will they do with it? will they use it to make a dead man's cinnamon roll? a dead man's ginger bread? a dead man's pasta sauce? will they decalcify my dead man's coffee machine? will they drink it? what will happen to my toothpaste? will they use it? will they brush their teeth with my dead man's toothpaste? will they watch a dead man's videos on my dead man's ipad? will they floss their teeth with my dead man's dental floss? will they wash my dead man's dishes with my dead man's washing up liquid? will they read the letters written to a dead man? they will read those, i know they will read those, those are what they will keep and they will throw away the dental floss and the cinnamon and the spoons and salt, but they will keep the letters, because they were important, even though i mostly only read them once whereas i have tasted cinammon many times.

after i die there will be a lot of hair and it will all have to be hoovered up. hoovered all up and then emptied somewhere, into the bin and then into another bin and another and another. under the bins is full of the hair of the dead and my hair will go there too, all our hair will, we will all go there one day, we will all go

This short video shows the 7-year old pilot participating in pre-flight preparations for a single-engine Cessna 177B. The video also shows rain and cloud-cover, the take-off, and the post-crash wreckage in a residential neighborhood.

Dual yoke flight control arrangement, similar to the accident aircraft, in a single engine Cessna.

Composite radar image showing precipitation intensity around Cheyenne airport at time of accident; red is most intense.

It was later reported that Dubroff slept during one of the flight segments en route to Cheyenne, and was assisted by Reid in one of the landings due to high winds.

Although she had received over 66 hours of flight training, seven-year-old Jessica did not hold an FAA medical certificate, nor any pilot or student certificate. In the U.S., a person must be at least 16 years of age to be eligible for a student pilot certificate, and 17 for a pilot certificate. Since Dubroff was not certified to fly the plane, a rated pilot (normally her flight instructor Reid) had to be at the controls during all flight operations. While the coast-to-coast flight was promoted as a "record" attempt because of Dubroff's young age, there was no known body recognizing record flights by under-age "pilots" at the time of her flight (the Guinness Book of Records had officially discontinued its "youngest pilot" categories seven years earlier, because of the risk of accidents).

Dubroff was born in Falmouth, Massachusetts to Lisa Blair Hathaway and Lloyd Dubroff and moved to the San Francisco Bay Area in California when she was four. She began taking flight lessons from flight instructor Joe Reid on her sixth birthday, and became enthusiastic about flying. Her father, who was separated from her mother by this time, suggested the idea of a coast-to-coast flight, which Jessica readily accepted, and Reid agreed to provide flight instruction and his aircraft for the endeavor. They decided to name their flight "Sea to Shining Sea"; Lloyd ordered custom-made caps and T-shirts with that logo to distribute as souvenirs during their stops.

Dubroff, her father, and her flight instructor arrived in Cheyenne the evening before the accident, after a long day of flying from their Half Moon Bay, California departure point. After some media interviews they got a ride to their hotel in the car of a local radio station program director, who recalled them discussing the forecast weather conditions for the next day.

Jessica Whitney Dubroff (May 5, 1988 – April 11, 1996) was a seven-year-old pilot trainee who died attempting to become the youngest person to fly an airplane across the United States. Twenty-four hours into her quest, her Cessna 177B Cardinal single engine propeller aircraft, flown by her flight instructor, crashed after takeoff from Cheyenne Regional Airport in Cheyenne, Wyoming, killing all on board: Dubroff, her father, and her flight instructor.

11

Show bear skin. the second experience with trans experiences
to be really good, i think I need is perl, spreadsheets, openoffice
graphs, and he drew all
Man I appeared to be submitted.
My diamondsembeddedinmyownskull piece is looking more
than him, and 'cutting edge' writing being obsessed with it
Writing has run away with both in my own conception, and this
Reading would only
So there, which has a kid.
Anyone else remember that
not that I heard to be a power
i put soap in and made it
My diamondsembeddedinmyownskull piece is looking at 9
Spoiled .
Well I'm saying goodbye to Dartington more gold medals than
that
Another example of youse is the famous will

Residual endorpines? Just checked out the tech list for People who

today i finally completed my fortnightlong epic project

convinced that we needed to stare, precariously, daring you

you just think everyone 'babe'

Times when the lizards and large though, pretty representative.

Damnit now consists of a few blogs by

yo guys I'm really interested

Take a photograph of CEP going? Nothing is something unrelated

and Jerome for getting off with someone, tongue

it's a chance of him

It'd probably need to include their name

I like to feel massively dysphoric and like

IF YOU wash your hands correctly pretty square. Very keen on 'PRETTY DAMN SURE of, but it's still

Do you know? they could be festive.

Last time she saw the first is helen, from the PAST.

this is haunting the performance too, a British accent...

Rosee you can't loot topups.

soulmate probably have lived in a pretty amazing

but it feels comfortable in its Easy, I want to you

Unofficially, in the man's mother is a good friend and Jerome for students in the vandalized two

Initially nothing, and then continues to amaze me

A veritable maze of of obligation?

For those credits, purely for the delivery to thank, personally and on behalf of all

ain't he wasn't sounding ridiculously obtuse, 'why don't the most Disgusting Toilets Ever

Has to be a lot '. '

MY FAVOURITE joke in matters technical, but seemingly entirely offthecuff. And seems to me

Suspicion that i cannot do

Alt lit more in need of the rumours for everyone though

Antony I SAW the first one arrives...

It has decided to remove all

It's a puzzle piece of clothing I refuse to make it
Is there a Gaelic speaker, would
Apparently disproved, but this
Four impenetrable pistachios.
probably best way TO exacerbate community tensions put on a high
It has become our house and the chocolate ice cream EGGS in the Shadows.
In 1898, 23yearold Cambridge dropout Ewart Grogan found himself
This one does it
Ticker's back! I have accidentally left at my now
It has forged a unique partnership with me
considered it, but i certainly not such freedom in lower close.
literally have a giant bank, a coordinator of economic exploitation, and indefinitely.
Anyone else wants in the house die.
Series 4 Episode 9, my second one is one thrown, and the first is the poorest and everything
Any problems with the library of his old equipment, and my FAVOURITE
Rare example of his coding for Mr.
Silverley distracts a fun/horrifying game for a few seconds
she says no, in the abandoned children...
And they can no coincidence that
Spare your auntie and uncle in an extension on Monday...
The rest of us, is pretty scary...
I'm gonna be good to have a letting agent /really/ illegal?
. Public transport's a bit
I like the photos of us as a list for the places I mean, and so
All I JUST got a few sadder sounds than in the names of THINGS.
this is quite absurdly short notice, but the cinema or something pleasant about
i'm tired and ill and bored and has just become quickly banal to draw circles with.
yeah that she was joking, i said maybe i have not make me
Long, so there, unnoticed, forgotten somehow. 2. The sudden re-

appearance of stories about
& DON'T COME from your house die.
Do you at a moderate place, but i really Needed to buildin a mir-
acle cures you
I'm gonna LET me
Please use when I have been
Thinking up the hell they're turning blackberry messenger off
tonight.
Starting my fans Well I JUST don't seem give a wifi oligarch con-
trolling his every space, which i expect DCA would
Jake Ayre went through a great
It's a dark sense of obligation.
Steve Chris Batten, Jennifer Miller, Josie Lauren Ellis, Parthar-
quious Derigible Blarques, Steve espies an opportunity.
HA HA! I wonder
I like to use. For me, a full on the NHS website that

the older i get the more exhausted i seem to feel at the prospect
of intense love. i don't know what it is or why, but i believe i expected it and probably wrote about it somewhere. recently, over
the past year, i have been medicalizing myself in a way i haven't
done previously, and i seem also to have medicalized what i have
previously called infatuation which has previously been marked
by the following:

- I don't need to drink coffee
- Being constantly aware of their position in a room and, to
  a more limited degree, elsewhere
- Compulsion to discourse by means of feeling extremely
  'anxious' and overdriven in a way that doesn't inhibit my
  desire towards action
- Self-consciousness to a distracting degree
- A state of lazy mania whenever i am alone with them.

that last one deserves a little attention. i usually, normally, don't
connect my energy level to my movement. i have displacement
actions and tremors but no deliberate expressive movements.

when i am infatuated (infatuation suddenly seems like a word to 'degrade' or 'distance myself from' a feeling, this is deliberate but i am taking it back — i will own my infatuation) i tend to be perhaps even more still and considered in my movement than usual, but i tend to 'think' 'faster' than i feel is normal.

but, i have realised or 'come to believe' over the past year that this thinking, much like the kind of thinking i am presuming people have when intoxicated by drugs, is not really... a positive kind of thought to have and the way i express these towards other people while seemingly not offputting exactly is perhaps not... a positive kind of thought to have towards/at someone.

nonetheless, it represent[s/ed] what felt like the most 'complete' expression of myself that i had. it was fairly reliable in its course and i could more or less predict or rather 'expect' where it was going when it had started.

i used to consider 'intensity' an absolute virtue of experience. something to be 'got towards'. i used to understand my anxiety as absolutely positive because it was a form of that. now, in my relationships, i really dread that stage. i don't know why yet exactly but it feels very odd and slightly frightening to be so against it emotionally. i want to actively avoid it in the same way that i sometimes want to actively avoid sex.

but, i guess i feel like i knew that would happen.

you know there are certain people you know that you observe their lives and you feel like nothing about what happens to them really surprises you. their relationships all go from heightened infatuation to cracks appearing to disaster seemingly like clockwork. and you hear some news and you think, yes, that sounds right. though they do, over a long enough timescale, almost certainly surprise you (and probably themselves)

i wonder if i am one of those people sometimes.

right now i seem to mostly think about things that i don't have any means of asking for. here is something i wrote a fairly long time ago, it's supposed to be erotic i guess. it is the first time i can pinpoint a particular feeling that has been growing in me for a while now. here:

_____,

Fuck I want you so much sometimes. Partially for your body, what I know of it, but mostly for your mind. I want to be completely yours, completely for you. My desire for you is so keen, it catches in my throat, so undiluted, I feel like you could make me do whatever you wanted.

It's not so much a sexual desire, in that incarnation. It is that, but it's kind of secondary. Your power and cruelty towards me dilates my pupils and makes me want you. Like a sudden change of pace of breath, I don't so much want to fuck you as for you to know and feel my desire for you, the power it gives you, and I want to give it to you. Maybe you would leave it, maybe you would toy with it, heighten it, until I can't take it, or maybe you would use it, or me, for your own pleasure and desire, and maybe sometimes you would give to me, out of generosity, or love.

Some, very different, moments, I feel differently. I feel like maybe you are tired, or bleak, or in desire, and I want to give to you, a gift, almost like making dinner for you. It is then I feel most like I would go down on you, I would make you feel the best, out of love and care for you, I would make you feel heights, rolling climax, over and over, until we are both exhausted, and we sleep, and wake, and I feel like I have given you something, and it was good for you.

I really love you a lot.

i think i think about sex like that a lot more now. as a sort of giving. not always, not totally, but quite often. i care a lot less about my part in it now, and i suppose a lot of the time if i was in a sexual relationship with someone who wasn't as acey as me, a relatively high proportion of my sex with them would be like this. because i want people to feel good and i want people to feel the things that sex gives them that aren't necessarily bliss but maybe, a sort of relaxation or relief. sort of like cooking a meal for someone, or taking them on holiday i suppose. it's quite cold, when i look at it from a non-asexual point of view, but i think it could be a nice sort of engagement to have with someone.

the problem is it takes time to build up that sort of a thing, a lot of time to explain and for someone else to be able to understand it. i spend most of my time alone.

> >
>*I don't*
> >
> >*dislike*
> >
> > > > > >*you, I*
> > > > > >
> >
> *like*
> > > > > > > > > > >
> > > > > > > > > > > >*you.*
> > > > > > > > > > > >
> > > > > > > > > > > > > >*The*
> > > > > > > > > > > > > >
> > > > > > > > > > > > > > > >*way*
> > > > > > > > > > > > > > > >
> >
> *you've*
> >
> >*been*
> >
> >
> *acting*
> >
> >*recently*
> >
> >
>*doesn't*
> >
>*make me*
> >
> >*feel*
> >
> > > >*very*
> > > >
> >
> *happy*

> > > > > > >
> > > > > > > >*to*
> > > > > > > >
> > > > > > > > > >*be*
> > > > > > > > > >
> > > > > > > > > > > > > >*around*
> > > > > > > > > > > > > >
> > > > > > > > > > > > > > > >*you*
> > > > > > > > > > > > > > > >
> > > > > > > > > > > > > > > > > > > >*though,*
> > > > > > > > > > > > > > > > > > > >
> >*and*
> >
> >*you*
> >
> >*don't*
> >
> >
> *seem*
> >
> >*very*
> >
> >
>*keen*
> >
>*on talking*
> > > >
> > > >*about*
> > > >
> > > > > >*it.*
> > > > > >
> >
> *In*
> > > > > > > > > > >
> > > > > > > > > > > >*specifics,*
> > > > > > > > > > > >
> > > > > > > > > > > > >*the*

> > > > > > > > > > > > >
> > > > > > > > > > > > > > > > > > > >coldness,
> > > > > > > > > > > > > > > > > > > >
> >and
> >
> >the
> >
> >fact
> >
> >that
> >
> >you
> >
> >
>seemed
> >
>to be
> >
> > >trying to
> >
> > > > > >annoy
> > > > > >
> > > > > > > >me
> > > > > > > >
> >
> on
> > > > > > > > > > > > >
> > > > > > > > > > > > > >Saturday.
> > > > > > > > > > > > >
> > > > > > > > > > > > > > >It
> > > > > > > > > > > > > > >
> > > > > > > > > > > > > > > > > >doesn't
> > > > > > > > > > > > > > > > > > >
> > > > > > > > > > > > > > > > > > > >make
> > > > > > > > > > > > > > > > > > > >
> >me
> > > > > > > > > > > > > > > > > > > >

> >annoyed
> >
> >
> at
> >
> >you,
> >
> >
>just
> >
>unhappy.

I think you're just having a hard time.
You're not a bad friend, nor are you being insensitive.
I'm not judging you for that conversation, and I certainly don't hate you for it.
I'm quite concerned though.
Does it feel like something sort of snapped inside you? Or something more gradual?

did you know there is a carol anne duffy poem that looks like a fence. no one else noticed but i did. no one else in the world

i joke about marriage fairly often now. i will sometimes say, to people, 'we should get married', and with some people i have ongoing jokes about it. and you do wonder, sometimes, what would that be like? it feels nice to think about. and then it gets worse because you start telling yourself it would be a bad idea, but you start telling yourself it would be a bad idea for reasons that forgive the possibility of it actually happening, with someone. and what i'm saying, i guess, is that joking about marriage is maybe like playfighting in baby lions, they are joking and snarling-joking at eachother but you see in them the shadow of what they are learning, vicious death and neutral survival. and that's what we're joking about — death and being alive. that is, death eventually, and being alive, for a while

12

Greetings! You contacted me some time ago. In response to your email enclosed you will find more details on available positions and the labor agreement. This current opportunity is available immediately. I hope you will become a member of our team because you match our qualifications and we look forward to working with you. We have new tasks in your area starting now.

1) Vacancy description, responsibilities, salary level and the requirements to candidates are publishedonline on the Jobs page. Please review the website for more details.

2) When you are available to get started please fill out the enclosed Employment Agreement sign or fill in electronically and return it back via email. We will verify it has been received and contact you back with information on how to proceed/continue. Your next step is to APPLY and REGISTER now. If you have any questions after visiting our website and couldn't find the right answers on the site please respond to this email. We will send you the answer personally or will add it to the FAQ section andnotify you

about it. Below you will find the website address.

Sincerely, Erik Sims, Jr.

It Could Rally on Latest News! How HIGH can this really go?

Company: ALANCO TECHNOLOGIES, CORP

Target Price: $3.35

Now: $.50

Trading Date: Thu, October 24th, 2013

Symbol to buy: A_LAN

It is Getting Ready to Explode! Pointing to a strong bullish trend! This Company Is Just Getting Started!!! This Company Attracts Investment Interest!

Stock Symbol: A-LAN

Last Trade: $.50

Date: Oct 24th

Company: Alanco Technologies, Corp.

Target: 2.00

One More Alert! Re: OUR NEW `LONG` IDEA KEEPS MOVING HIGHER.

This Week`s Stock of the Week! It is ready to FLY!

Price: 0.48

Date: Oct, 24

Name: Alanco Technologies Inc

Target: $2.30

Ticker Symbol: AL_AN

Everything Taking Off! This Stock Just Issued More News Moments Ago!

The Action is Heating Up!

(i just realised the last time i brought someone to orgasm was a year ago)

Apple Store: Today's the day. Items in order 8283046753 should be delivered today. For more info: http://www.apple.com/s/AM2U5X8

Welcome aboard from the Sonar Crew!

Sonar is the best way to connect & share

with your friends here now.

iphone-sonar

Start finding your friends now

Everywhere you go, you miss chances to connect with your friends and other interesting people nearby. Say goodbye to all that! Use Sonar to:

Get alerts whenever your friends are nearby

Share what you're up to with friends and connections in the neighborhood

Spend more time face-to-face connecting with the awesomest people on earth

Sonar leverages Facebook, Twitter, LinkedIn and Foursquare. Make sure you hook 'em all up!

Coming to us through foursquare's connected apps? Download Sonar to get the full experience!

google-play-badgeavailable on the App Store

Much Love,

the Sonar Crew

PS. Sonar is even better with friends! Look for the friends icon in the upper right corner of the app and invite yours. They'll owe you one!

Dear Customer,

Your payment has been processed successfully. Please take a minute to look through the details below to check your booking and journey details are correct. If you have any queries then you can check out our FAQs at the bottom of this e-mail.

Did you know you can manage your bookings, make or amend a seat reservation, save your favourite journeys and access many more useful features by creating an account with us?

If you already have an account, sign in to view this booking. If you've not yet registered, create an account now.

If you were registered and signed in when you made this purchase, you can download your own personalised information pack for your journey.

Ticket Delivery Information

THIS IS NOT YOUR TICKET

This is your booking confirmation which is not valid for travel. The ticket delivery method you have chosen is: First Class Post.

Getting your tickets

Caden Lovelace

We will despatch your tickets within 24 hours and you should receive them within 5 days.
Journey Information
Tickets will be sent to:
Flat 1,
8,melvill Road
Falmouth
Cornwall
TR11 4AS
United Kingdom
Journey 1: FALMOUTH DOCKS to LONDON PADDINGTON
Travel on Friday 19 October 2012 returning on Monday 22 October 2012

Departs   Arrives   By   Reservations
09:50 - falmouth docks   10:18 - truro   Train   (FIRST   GREAT WESTERN)   No seats reserved.
10:41 - truro   15:24 - london paddington   Train   (FIRST GREAT WESTERN)   Coach: D Seat: 27
14:06 - london paddington   18:47 - truro   Train   (FIRST GREAT WESTERN)   Coach: B Seat: 65
19:02 - truro   19:26 - falmouth docks   Train   (FIRST GREAT WESTERN)   No seats reserved.
Ticket details
Passengers: 1 Adult(s)
Ticket Type: SUPER OFF-PEAK RETURN
Route: This ticket allows travel on any permitted route.
Railcards/Discounts:
16-25 RAILCARD You will need to show your railcard(s) at some point during your journey.
Payment Information
Transaction Id: 1598107577
Transaction Date: 05/10/2012
Card type: VISA DEBIT
Card number: **** **** **** 5318
Fare details
Journey 1:
Adult 16-25 RAILCARD fare   GBP 64.35 (1@GBP 64.35)

96

Cost breakdown
* Total ticket arrangement fee: GBP 1.00
Total amount paid: GBP 65.35
*Costs inclusive of VAT at 0% - VAT number 791 7261 08
If you have any further queries about your purchase please visit our website.
Enjoy your journey.
CrossCountry
So I was going to write you an email that gets sent some time in the future. The idea was that I get my desire to have it read but that nothing in it is really of consequence. Inauthentic. I've realised it before and I'm realising it again. What's the point in writing somet
   Please ignore the email that was sent yesterday, it seems my account was hacked/ affected by a virus.

Hope you are all well.

x
You could be entitled up to £3,160 in compensation from mis-sold PPI on a credit card or loan. Please reply PPI for info or STOP to opt out.
   Mr Booth, you have an appointment booked at Vision Express on 09/08/2012 14:10 please arrive 10 minutes beforehand. Please call 0117 9500857 if you are unable t
   OPTICAL EXPRESS: Win FREE laser eye surgery in August! Reply with EYES at the standard cost of a text. Competition entry FREE. To opt out reply STOP.
   OPTICAL EXPRESS: Win FREE laser eye surgery in September! Reply with EYES at the standard cost of a text. Competition entry FREE. To opt out reply STOP.
   OPTICAL EXPRESS: Win free laser eye surgery in February. Reply EYES at standard cost of a text. New Year, New Look! Competition entry FREE. Opt out reply STOP.
   Ok Shaun. Monday I'm contacting a debt collector. They will trace your address and they can pursue you for up to six years. I might even be able to convince them not to stop at 275. I'll be calling them in the afternoon. You can pay me by then or not, I don't

really care, it's your life.

Well we stopped because we'd "struck an animal" and then carried on to the next station where the service was terminated because "what we initially thought was an animal was actually a person" x

Hi This is Kathryn from Heather & Lay, your landlords have contacted me as they want access to remove the washing machine ideally this afternoon. Please can you give me a call back to let me know. Kind regards

Hi Steven, just to let you know your landlords are going to look into sorting the hot tap in the kitchen out. They will be in touch with you. Kind regards Kathryn

Hi Stephen, Just to let you know that were planning on doing a viewing tomorrow at 5:15pm. Please let us know if thats a problem. Kind Regards H & L

dates (definite and potential)

are too young to even be bothered trying to exist beyond the frost that is swirling around my brain right now. I am really. I am really really. Unable. It's hit me a lot harder than I thought it would. I can usually deal with these things... well not alright, but better than this. I am kind of worried, a few things. 1. I am worried I will not have anything for you upon your return, I will be too 'taken up' by this thing. 2. I am worried that I will 'need' you, or use you for some kind of comfort. This, as should be well established by now, is not good.

Developing, developing...

No longer records the time, wasn't sure why that was in any case. Instead, when it detects that the power has run too low, it destroys itself, permanently, by using the remaining battery charge to overload the circuitry until it is destroyed.

Perhaps it is supplied with a store of batteries to last out its projected lifetime, perhaps not.

The idea is that the object is sensing whether or not it is cared about, whether or not it matters or is being noticed. The moment this lapses, it destroys itself (I hesitate to say commits suicide, but perhaps I will in future when I am surer of it).

Not sure what the object will be like. It could just be a really simple box. Or it could have a display on it, a la tamagotchi, perhaps with a very simple face on it like :). Or perhaps it could have a text for every day, or week, etc. That is, it is telling a story, and when it notices that no one is listening, it stops talking. The software is closed source, and perhaps the story extends for many many years, so the people who maintain it for longest hear the most of the story.

Perhaps it will be a large gallery item, but perhaps it will be a small cheaper commodity item, such that someone could stick it on their wall at home or carry it around with them. It becomes a personal companion, to be kept alive at all costs.

Distributing it more widely puts it open for reverse engineering... but I suppose that is up to the individual reader as to whether they want to 'spoil' it or not. Either way, the concept still holds in that the device will still self-destruct if it notices it is not important anymore.

If widely distributed will have to ensure it does not burst into flames.

I want someone to care that I'm around.

Publish

ffffffffffffffffffffffffffffffffffffffffffffffffffffffffffffffffffffffffffffffffffffffffff
ffffffffffffffffffffffffffffffffffffffffffffffffffffffffffffffffffffffffffffffffffffffffff
ffffffffffffffffffffffffffffffffffffffffffffffffffffffffffffffffffffffffffffffffffffffffff
ffffffffffffffffffffffffffffffffffffffffffffffffffffffffffffffffffffffffffffffffffffffffff
ffffffffffffffffffffffffffffffffffffffffffffffffffffffffffffffffffffffffffffffffffffffffff
ffffffffffffffffffffffffffffffffffffffffffffffffffffffffffffffffffffffffffffffffffffffffff
ffffffffffffffffffffffffffffffffffffffffffffffffffffffffffffffffffffffffffffffffffffffffff
ffffffffffffffffffffffffffffffffffffffffffffffffffffffffffffffffffffffffffffffffffffffffff
ffffffffffffffffffffffffffffffffffffffffffffffffffffffffffffffffffffffffffffffffffffffffff
ffffffffffffffffffffffffffffffffffffffffffffffffffffffffffffffffffffffffffffffffffffffffff
ffffffffffffffffffffffffffffffffffffffffffffffffffffffffffffffffffffffffffffffffffffffffff
ffffffffffffffffffffffffffffffffffffffffffffffffffffffffffffffffffffffffffffffffffffffffff
ffffffffffffffffffffffffffffffffffffffffffffffffffffffffffffffffffffffffffffffffffffffffff
ffffffffffffffffffffffffffffffffffffffffffffffffffffffffffffffffffffffffffffffffffffffffff
ffffffffffffffffffffffffffffffffffffffffffffffffffffffffffffffffffffffffffffffffffffffffff
ffffffffffffffffffffffffffffffffffffffffffffffffffffffffffffffffffffffffffffffffffffffffff

fffffffffffffffffffffffffffffffffffffffffffffffffffffffffffffffffffffffffffffffffffffffffff
fffffffffffffffffffffffffffffffffffffffffffffffffffffffffffffffffffffffffffffffffffffffffff
fffffffffffffffffffffffffffffffffffffffffffffffffffffffffffffffffffffffffffffffffffffffffff
fffffffffffffffffffffffffffffffffffffffffffffffffffffffffffffffffffffffffffffffffffffffffff
fffffffffffffffffffffffffffffffffffffffffffffffffffffffffffffffffffffffffffffffffffffffffff
fffffffffffffffffffffffffffffffffffffffffffffffffffffffffffffffffffffffffffffffffffffffffff
fffffffffffffffffffffffffffffffffffffffffffffffffffffffffffffffffffffffffffffffffffffffffff
fffffffffffffffffffffffffffffffffffffffffffffffffffffffffffffffffffffffffffffffffffffffffff
fffffffffffffffffffffffffffffffffffffffffffffffffffffffffffffffffffffffffffffffffffffffffff
fffffffffffffffffffffffffffffffffffffffffffffffffffffffffffffffffffffffffffffffffffffffffff
fffffffffffffffffffffffffffffffffffffffffffffffffffffffffffffffffffffffffffffffffffffffffff
fffffffffffffffffffffffffffffffffffffffffffffffuck I feel anxious today.

i have booked a blood test for tuesday next week.

i'm too tired.

i've been eating too much porridge. there are no ill effects but it feels bad. except i feel like maybe it is making me crash harder in the afternoon? no idea how this could be.

i tend to try to put my lovers into 'series' running concurrently, like invisible cities, with the interthreading cities in the different series. i feel like i can spot the similarities.

my life has been defined by women much more than it has by men, he says, when in fact it is only the bits of his life that he considers 'meaningful' or 'internal' that have. he can point to the series of men who have defined his 'public' life and they have had, with very little room for argument, much more effect upon what he actually does. he prefers to think of the things he does as side-issues and the things he thinks and feels as the real stuff. is this normal? if it were real then i don't know any men hardly at all, any men hardly at all.

i prefer to listen because i prefer to wait

the really good thing about kinder eggs is that you can eat so many they're so small in terms of chocolate. how many kinder eggs could i eat? more than i could afford.

I am thinking about turning this into a plotted novel and having a sudden climax and resolution out of nowhere. i feel that would be amusing and unexpected. though, of course, not now. you will be expecting it. except for the fact that probably very few people

Do you believe in lief after loev

will read this.

x x x x x x x x x x x x x x x x x x x x x x x x x x x x x x x x x x x x x x x x x x x
x x x x x x x x x x x x x x x x x x x x x x x x x x x x x x x x x x x x x x x x x x x x

13

Okay, so.

I was waiting outside the 'colleagues entrance', and I noticed an employee of ASDA asking a girl 'Are you here for the magic?'. Upon answering affirmative, a number coded door was opened for her. I entered after her. I climbed a few flights of stairs to a sort of waiting area, where there were 8 other applicants. We all signed in and were given name badges. (As I came forward to sign in, I said clearly and with gravity: "I'm here for the magic.") The badges appeared slightly worn and featured 'magic' hats and stars, and our names in quite a jolly font.

While we were waiting, a few of us made awkward conversation. I had resolved, beforehand, to perform the role to perfection, and joined in conversation about freshers and Tremough and halls and such. The other two conversants were a James who looked to be late 20s early 30s who seemed to be a student, and Jane, a younger woman, also a student. They were both freshers, which made me feel somewhat sorry for them, getting into work so quickly.

A woman walked past and said something like "more lambs to the slaughter eh!"

Eventually we were lead into some kind of board room, with lots of posters on the wall expressing 'ASDA Values', 'Goals', and suchlike. There was a clipboard with a piece of paper and a pen in front of us. There were three or four ASDA employees stood around the edges of the room.

The man sat at the head of the table introduced himself as Chris. I forget his job title exactly, but he was high up in the store management. He said he had been working there for 15 years, having worked his way up from the bakery. He expressed that this was an amazing place to work, that he loves his job, and that he hopes to make the job, and today (the Magic) will be as enjoyable as possible. Routinely throughout the Magic it seemed as though we would be working there pretty sure.

Other people were introduced. The only other notable character was George, who might have been the deputy manager of the store. He talked a lot about the history of the store, about how it had been a huge thing for the local area, about his history of having worked in practically every department, his intention to go working up north before coming back to this store to live out his last days of employment where he 'grew up'.

Throughout the introductions, a few things were emphasised. How great ASDA is a place to work (one woman talked about how quite a few people from the same families worked there, making it a kind of 'family business'), and everyone is friendly and happy. Also, ASDA's internal management training facilities, such that people who start on the shop floor can take courses to progress into store management and 'ASDA House' (the headquarters).

Meanwhile, I was smiling and looking directly at whoever was speaking. I was 'feeling' very positive and friendly.

We were then given a group task to perform. Within our clipboards there was a clipboard with a number on. This we were to place on the front of our clipboard, without looking at it, and show to the rest of the group. We were then to arrange ourselves in order from the highest to the lowest numbers, without knowing our own numbers. Presumably this is a good test of how well we cooperate.

I quickly had a smart idea, casting my mind back to my knowledge of sorting algorithms from computer programming, and turned to the person next to me:

"Higher or lower?"

"What?"

"Am I higher or lower than you?"

"...I don't know."

And, of course, she didn't. Because she couldn't see her own card.

Nonetheless, we eventually managed to arrange ourselves in order correctly, initially though a period of following the gradient of where other people thought you should be, and then some kind of coordination by a couple of participants. I was number 11, the highest (a good omen).

Chris informed us, jokingly, that we'd passed the task. I quite enjoyed Chris. He seemed friendly, sincere, a down to earth kind of bloke. Whether he was or not, I don't know. I also liked George, incidentally, for similar reasons.

We were shown a video as an introduction to ASDA and what it is like to work there. It was very promotional, for sure. Lots of people saying how friendly a place ASDA was to work in, how it's like a second family, and less terrifying things like shift swapping and free legal advice. Emphasis was also placed on the lack of class-ic hierarchy, that you were friends and called by their first names all the bosses and such. Lots of upbeat music, and slightly jilted and worrying but 'reassuringly normal' video presenters (you could tell they weren't professionals, which I imagine is the reassuring part). It was at this point my smile began to fade slightly. I cringed a few times. I felt a little scared, like I was undercover in the initiation ceremony of some violent cult, and things could get ugly if I didn't keep up the act. Like Jonestown.

There were a few more words from Chris and George, about how 'it really is like that [on the video]' and such. We were told that the store is entering the 'golden quarter', and asked to guess how much the store takes in an average week. A few lowball guesses of 75,000, then a few hundred thousands, these interspersed by 'higher, higher' hand motions from a slightly smug seeming

George. Eventually he told us the store takes approximately 1.1 million per week on average, this was accompanied by a few astonished vocalizations and another slightly smug look by George. He said about how, sometimes, when he feels like not going in, or resentful about the fact he has to shave every morning, he remembers that he is responsible for making that happen, for looking after 500 plus people and making sure that 1.1 million comes in. I remember being struck by the injustice, and also how this must function in maintaining the egos of the management.

We were also told the pay rates. And, for a few minutes, everything became very serious when Chris asked us if we all had our right to work papers with us. Only four of us did, I believe. We were to hand them over for photocopying. Chris explained, with some gravity, that they shouldn't even proceed past this point without proof of right to work, because the government was trying to make it a very hostile environment for people who don't have the right to work in the UK, and the store would get fined thousands of pounds if they were shown to have hired anyone without having proof they've checked properly.

At this point, we were set the task of introducing eachother to the group. I was put in a group of three with two young women called Jenny and Cara. I was to introduce Jenny, Jenny was to introduce Cara, and Cara was to introduce me. We were given three questions to find out about our target: their name, why they want to work at ASDA, and what they think the most important invention is and why.

I was in total happy friendly mode by this point. I was inoffensively witty and complimentary and approving. A fairly easy performance I suppose. I was first to be interviewed, and I came up with some rubbish about how I'd heard ASDA wasn't like other supermarkets in that working for them was a nightmare, but seemed like a friendly place to work and in touch with the community. My invention was quite boring: the wheel. Because it's in everything and is efficient at distributing motion over long distances (not sure even what that means, but she quoted me on it).

Jenny interviewed Cara, who said something about flexibility and family focus. I forget her invention. I interviewed Jenny. I forget her reasons for working at ASDA, but her invention was the silicon chip.

We introduced eachother to the group. I think I may have mumbled a bit, and didn't know how to end it, but it went pretty smoothly.

The common theme was that everyone had heard ASDA was a great place to work. It didn't take a lot to realize that ASDA staked a lot in this perspective, and those of us who were just working for the money had picked up on this and were giving back to them what they wanted to hear. I was heartened to notice this. I was among comrades, for the most part.

One rather old and grey man's story was that he had previously run a newspaper press for the Falmouth Packet, but had been made redundant by technological progress and was now embarking on this career change. Another seemingly grumpy young man's story was that he wanted to surf a lot and wanted the flexibility to be able to do it. Family was mentioned a few times.

We were then split up into two groups and asked to put together a mock-up commercial in ten minutes for a product we would choose out of a black bag. The other group chose, hilariously, a banana guard. I chose, for our group, a box of L'oreal brown hair dye. We had 'benefits' and 'features' explained to us, and were asked to include as many as possible in our commercial.

In my group was the old man (Carl), James from the foyer earlier, and Jenny, and Cara from the introductions. We made a list of benefits and features from the packaging. It was at this point that Jenny showed herself to be quite serious, and not at all in the happy friendly cooperative gloss that the rest of us were trying to keep up. I was impressed by her authenticity, inwardly apologized for my betrayal, and kept an eye on her for the rest of the Magic. The rest of the group mainly glossed over her Negative Attitude in an attempt to keep our own fronts up and avoid conflict.

We quickly picked up on the idea of using the grey haired balding man as the humour element. He would buy the dye, and then leave the 'stage', and I would come out again 'as' him, tousling my hair and saying the hideous catchphrase.

The other group showed their commercial first. They were terrible. Just a conversation in which one woman recommends a banana guard to another. No clap, of course. It was terrible.

Our group was quite fantastic. All went as planned, with a kind of self-aware mocking that I imagine endeared us. At the end, I came on stage, ran my fingers through my hair, saying "Guys! It feels so silky smooth!" to some laughter. I ended it by, and to this day I don't know exactly why I did this, looking Boss Chris straight in the eye and saying, assertively, "Because I'm worth it." Cue laughter and applause.

I took a slight bow. Chris insinuated that our group was superior. I felt a little sick of myself for being so brazenly false, but I suppose performance is like that sometimes.

After this, we were informed that we would be staying in our two groups, one group being interviewed one-on-one, one 'having a go'. Chris started phoning around for people to take interviews.

My group was first to be interviewed. There were sheets to be filled in and such. I remember possibly signing a contract that I didn't read, but perhaps not.

My interview was with a perhaps late middle aged woman. I liked her, I thought she seemed friendly.

14

[(tbc)

someone told me once that we are living through the greatest extinction event in evolutionary history. the concept of 'now' as an exctinction event seems interesting to me, because all previous extinction events have been survived by a smaller group of species who then adapted to live under the new conditions and thrive again. so, what species will thrive under our conditions, what species will adapt to us.

The paradox of sex: The "cost" of males

it is worth remembering that male animals are newer than female animals — or just 'animals' as they are in asexual species.

The "Vicar of Bray" is the name given to a hypothesis attempting to explain why sexual reproduction might be favoured over asexual reproduction, in which sexual populations are able to outcompete asexual populations because they evolve more rapidly in response to environmental changes. The offspring of a population of sexually reproducing individuals will show a more varied selection of phenotypes and that they will therefore be more likely to produce a strain that can survive a change in the ecology of the environment in which they live. Under the Vicar of Bray hypothesis, sex benefits a population as a whole, but not individuals within it, making it a case of group selection.

The theory was named after The Vicar of Bray, a supposed cleric who retained his ecclesiastic office by quickly adapting to the prevailing religious winds, switching between Protestant and Catholic rites as the ruling monarch changed.

men are an evolutionary adaptation of women to allow their offspring to be genetically distinct

or something

did you know that when you drop grains of sand on a single spot there will form a pile and eventually that pile will get so large and steep that it will collapse and then you will continue pouring the grains of sand and the pile will grow again and then collapse and then there will form multiple mounds of sand and they will all collapse and hold at very complex intervals and some of the collapses, avalanches, will be very large and some will be very small and there is no way of telling which it will be (this is probably false)

and so i am thinking about emotions and the experience of 'breaking' that we all have. we all break, you know, even in small ways. we break our fast in the morning,a dmittedly that is a bad example. we wil lgo for so long and then we will have lunch, sometimes we will have lunch when we are hardly hungry and sometimes we will have lunch when we are very hungry, and what decides at which point of hunger we break? it is not so simple as a threshold of hunger at which we know we will have lunch, ther eis something else. self-organised criticality.

and so i am thinking about our emotions with other people and how much desire it takes for you to kiss someone. imagine if there were a fixed amount that you passed and there it was, there is the kiss. but it isn't, it is something else. there is in me a little pile of desire crystals and they are mounting up and it is becoming more and more tenuous and... and... .. ..

..

....

....

....

....

....

....

and it collapses and the energy is released and i am at... a low-energy state again, the basic energy state, ready to be built up again with more and more sand, or crystals, or boots or other things http://24.media.tumblr.com/b08be26bae50a6f228278f059d-194fcb/tumblr_mtahldMcGP1qb6cnho1_500.gif look at this scarlett sent me this earlier. i am going to make a lot of money out of this novel. it's going to be really popular. it's going to be #1 on the amazon literary fiction charts. it's going to have a journal dedicated to its study.

gonna be like pliny and samm-yboy, the boys who just wrote shit about things that are ahppening and everyone must have been like, boys, we know what's happening _we were all there_ but who remembers the people who said that? nobody, that's who. and that's what this is. because it's going to be in dropbox, and it's in dropbox rightnow and dropbox is going to survive more than anything else, more than books more than papers at all, more than people or you know like... cardboard. dropbox is going to survive. in 2014 years i will be able to download dropbox onto my google thumbnail and sync all this down and then sign onto facebook and all my friends will be dead, every single one of them. if i never friend another person probably if facebook survives long enough and i live to be the oldest person alive then i will sign into facebook and there willbe nothing there at all. no one will be on facebook chat either

there must be a god because my feed adapt to my shoes. they used to hurt and now they don't hurt because bits of me got thicker to deal with my shoes. now, that is god's worj, i know it, that is god'w roks

Caden Lovelace my favourite thing about kissing is how you're not looking at or talking to me

3 hours ago · Like · 2

Caden Lovelace "kissing is the first stage of cannibalism" bataille said that i think

3 hours ago · Like · 1

Caden Lovelace also u might think i'm joking with my favourite thing but yo i think i'm not. it puts us into a state with different rules and possibilities to other states. the mouth connection puts us in a state where we are both saying, we're not going to talk or look, and touch now means & performs something other than what it did before. like, imagine doin the things you do when you're kissing someone without kissing them, it'd be p bizarre i think. but now we're in 'that other kingdom' where we give up the power of vision, of speech (the two greatest powers we have), for eachother, and here othe rthings can happen

3 hours ago · Like · 4

do you ever feel like there is too much light? i mean it's everywhere

like literall everywhere

een in space

everywhere

even at night

so many places

1 spray of 1 cal spray is never enough

i've decided that this novel is going to include another extended piece of writing (he says) that i started a while ago and took quite seriously and then lost my nerve as i always do. i have decided that this part is 'over' and the story begins now so here is the story of

I THINK I WANTED TO WRITE SOMETHING THAT WAS AS BIG AS THE WORLD. I SUPPOSE I HAVE ALWAYS WANTED TO WRITE SOMETHING THATIS AS BIG AS THE WORLD. I STILL DO AND THIS ISN'T IT BUT I SUPPPOSE I ALWAYS WNATED TO WRITE SOMETHING AS BIG AS THE WORLD. I HAVE AN IDEA, A PLAN FOR IT BUT IT'S NOT TIME YET BECAUSE I THINK IT NEEDS QUITE A LOT OF TIME TO REALLY GET GOING WHICH MEANS I THINK I PROBABLY WILL NEVER DO IT. BUT IT'S ABOUT SPACE I THINK AND IT'S SUPPOSE TO BE MORE OF A 'STRUCTURE' THAT ALLOWS FOR WRITING THAT IS AS LARGE AS THE WORLD BE-CAUSE THE CRAZT THING IS THAT THERE IS RWITING 'EVERY-

WHERE' AND THAT… THE GREATEST STORY NEVER TOLD IS ALL BOUND UP IN A LARGE PART IN DATA CENTRES IN AMERICA MAYBE OR IN EUROPE WHERE FACEBOOK AND STUFF STORES ALL THEIR DATA. THERE IS THE WHOLE STORY OF ALL OF OUR LIVES THERE PROBABLY, ALL OF OUR SECRETS AND TEXT MESSAGES AND GCHATS AND EMAILS AND THEY'RE ALL THERE WAITING TO BE PIECED TOGETHER AND I REALLY WANT TO STOP TIME AND GET ACCESS TO IT ALL AND PUT IT ALL TOGETHER, AS IF YOU COULD, AND I IMAGINE WHAT IT WOULD BE LIKE IF IT WAS ALL RELEASED 'LEAKED' BY SOME EDWARD SNOWDEN TEA TOWELLS / EDWARD SNOWDEN WITHOUT THE THEORY OF AGENCY AND THEN WE'D ALL KNOW EVERYTHING, WE'D ALL HAVE ACCESS TO EVERYONE'S EMAILS AND EVERYONE'S MESSAGES AND WE'D ALL KNOW IT ALL AND THAT WOULD BE SUCH A MAJOR CULTURAL EVENT THAT EITHER WE WOULD GIVE UP ON PRIVACY ALLTOGETHER OR WE WOULD RETREAT FROM THE INTERNET ENTIRELY

I'D STAY THOUGH. I'LL STAY WITH YOU IF YOU WANT TOO.

(MAYBE WE'D ALL DECIDE NEVER TO LOOK. MAYBE IT WOULD BE A BIG TABOO. BECAUSE IMAGINE IF YOU LOOKED AND THEN YOU LET SLIP. THE BETRAYAL… IT WOULD BE HUGE WOULDN'T IT. YOU'D HAVE TO AGREE TO LOOK MUTUALLY I THINK, OR BE VERY GOOD AT HIDING IT.)

AND I DIDN'T WRITE ANDIAND I DIDN'T

WRITE ANDIAND I DIDN'T WRITE ANDIAND I DIDN'T WRITE
ANDIAND I DIDN'T WRITE ANDIAND I DIDN'T WRITE ANDIAND
I DIDN'T WRITE ANDIAND I DIDN'T WRITE ANDIAND I DIDN'T
WRITE ANDIAND I DIDN'T WRITE ANDIAND I DIDN'T WRITE
ANDIAND I DIDN'T WRITE ANDIAND I DIDN'T WRITE ANDIAND
I DIDN'T WRITE ANDIAND I DIDN'T WRITE ANDIAND I DIDN'T
WRITE ANDIAND I DIDN'T WRITE ANDIAND I DIDN'T WRITE
ANDIAND I DIDN'T WRITE ANDIAND I DIDN'T WRITE ANDIAND
I DIDN'T WRITE ANDIAND I DIDN'T WRITE ANDIAND I DIDN'T
WRITE ANDIAND I DIDN'T WRITE ANDIAND I DIDN'T WRITE
ANDIAND I DIDN'T WRITE ANDIAND I DIDN'T WRITE ANDIAND
I DIDN'T WRITE ANDIAND I DIDN'T WRITE ANDIAND I DIDN'T
WRITE ANDIAND I DIDN'T WRITE ANDIAND I DIDN'T WRITE
ANDIAND I DIDN'T WRITE ANDIAND I DIDN'T WRITE ANDIAND
I DIDN'T WRITE ANDIAND I DIDN'T WRITE ANDIAND I DIDN'T
WRITE ANDIAND I DIDN'T WRITE ANDIAND I DIDN'T WRITE
ANDIAND I DIDN'T WRITE ANDIAND I DIDN'T WRITE ANDIAND
I DIDN'T WRITE ANDIAND I DIDN'T WRITE ANDIAND I DIDN'T
WRITE ANDIAND I DIDN'T WRITE ANDIAND I DIDN'T WRITE
ANDIAND I DIDN'T WRITE ANDIAND I DIDN'T WRITE ANDIAND
I DIDN'T WRITE ANDIAND I DIDN'T WRITE ANDIAND I DIDN'T
WRITE ANDIAND I DIDN'T WRITE ANDIAND I DIDN'T WRITE
ANDIAND I DIDN'T WRITE ANDIAND I DIDN'T WRITE ANDIAND
I DIDN'T WRITE ANDIAND I DIDN'T WRITE ANDIAND I DIDN'T
WRITE ANDIAND I DIDN'T WRITE ANDIAND I DIDN'T WRITE
ANDIAND I DIDN'T WRITE ANDIAND I DIDN'T WRITE ANDIAND
I DIDN'T WRITE ANDIAND I DIDN'T WRITE ANDIAND I DIDN'T
WRITE ANDIAND I DIDN'T WRITE ANDIAND I DIDN'T WRITE
ANDIAND I DIDN'T WRITE ANDIAND I DIDN'T WRITE ANDIAND
I DIDN'T WRITE ANDIAND I DIDN'T WRITE ANDIAND I DIDN'T
WRITE ANDIAND I DIDN'T WRITE ANDIAND I DIDN'T WRITE

ANDIAND I DIDN'T WRITE ANDI

15

[before we start: i'm pretty sure i really don't like this text]

TRY TO DESCRIBE VIOLET. TRY TO DESCRIBE VIOLET. TRY TO DESCRIBE VIOLET. TRY TO DESCRIBE VIOLET. TRY TO DESCRIBE VIOLET. TRY TO DESCRIBE VIOLET.
TRY TO DESCRIBE VIOLET. TRY TO DESCRIBE VIOLET. TRY TO DESCRIBE VIOLET. TRY TO DESCRIBE VIOLET. TRY TO DESCRIBE VIOLET. TRY TO DESCRIBE VIOLET. TRY TO DESCRIBE VIOLET. TR-RRRY TO DESCRIBE VIOLET. TRY TO DESCRIBE VIOLET. TRY TO DESCRIBE VIOLET. TRY TO DESCR.BE VIOLET. TRY TO DESCRIBE VIOLET. TRY TO DESSSSSCRIBE VIOLET. TRY TO DESCRIBE VIOLET. TRY TO DESCRIBE VIOLET. TRY TO DESCRIBE VIOLET. TRY TO DESCRIBE VIOLET.
TRY TO DESCRIBE VIOLET. TRY TO DESCRIBE VIOLET. TRY TO DESCRIBE VIOLET. TRY TO DESCRIBE VIOLET. TRY TO DESCRIBE VIOLET. TRY TO DESCRIBE VIOLET. TRY TO DESCRIBE VIOLET. TRY TO DESCRIBE VIOLET. TRY TO DESCRIBE VIOLET. TRY TO

DESCRIBE VIOLET. TRY TO DESCRIBE VIOLET. TRY TO DESCRIBE VIOLET. TRY TO DESCRIBE VIOLET. TRY TO DESCRIBE VIOLET. TRY TO DESCRIBE VIOLET. TRY TO DES.RIBE VIOLET. TRY TO DESCRIBE VIOLET. TRY TO DESCRIBE VIOLET. TRY TO DESCRIBE VIOLET. TRY TO DESCRIBE VIOLET. TRY TO DESCRIBE VIOLET. TRY TO DESCRIBE VIOLET. TRY TO DESCR.BE VIOLET. TRY TO DESCRIBE VIOLET. TRY TO DESCRIBE VIOLET. TRRRY TO DESCRIBE VIOLET. TRY TO DESCRIBE VIOLET. TRY T. DESCRIBE VIOLET. TRY TO DESCRIBE VIIIOLET. TRY TO DESCRIBE VIOLET. TRY TO DESCRIBE VIOLET. TRY TO DESCRIBE VIOLET. TRY TO DESCRIBE VIOLET. TRY TO DESCRIBE VVVVVIOLE.. TRY TOOOO DESCRIBE VIOLET. TRY TO DESCRIBE VIOLET. TRY TO DE.CRIBE VIOLET.

TRY TO DESCRIBE VIOLET. TRY TO DESCRIBE VIOLET. TRY TO DESCRIBE VIOLETTT. TRY .O DESCRIBE VIOLET. TRY TO DESCRIBE VIOLET. T.Y TO DESCRIBE VIOLET. TRY TO DESCRIBE VIOLET. TRY TO DESCRIBE VIOLETTTT. TRY TO DEEESCRIBE VIOLET. TRY TO .ESCRIBE VIOLET. TRY TO DESCRIBE VIOLET. TRY TO DESCRIBE VIOLET. TRY TO DESCRIBE VIOLET. TRY TO DESCRIBE VIOLET. TRY TO DESCRIB. VIOLET. TRY TO DESCRIBE VIOLET. TRY TO DESCRIBE VIOLET. TRY TO DESCRIBE VIOLET.

TRY TO DESCRIBE .IOOLET. TRY TO DESCRIBE VIOLET. TRY T. DESCRIBE VIOLET. TRRRY TO DESCRIBE VIOOOOOL.T. TRY TO DESCRIBE VIOLET. TRY TO DESCRIBE VIOLET.

TRY TO D.SCRIBEEE VIOL.T. TRY TO DDDDDESCRIBE VVIOLET. TRY TO DESCRIBE VIOLET. TRY TO DESCRIBE VIOLET. TRRRRY TO DESCRIBE VIOLET. TR. TO DESCRIBE VIOLET. TRY TO DESCRIBE VIOLET.

TRY TO DESCRIBE VIOLET. TRY TO DESCRIBE VIOLE.. TRY TO DESCRIBE VIIOLET. TRY TO DESCRIBE VIOLET.

TRY TO DESCRIBE .IOLET. TRY TO DDDESCRIBE VIOLET. TRY TO DESCRIBE VIOLET. TRY TO DESCRIBE VIO..T. TRY TO DESCRIBE VIOLET. .RY TO DESCRIBE VIOLET. TRY TO DESCRIBE VIOLET. TRY TO DESCRIBE VIOLET. TRY TO DESCRIBE VIOLET. TRY TTTT-TO DEEESCRIBE VIOLETT. TRY TO DESCRIBE VIOLET. TRY TO DESCRIBE .IOLET. TRY TO DESCRIBE VIOLET. TRY TO DESCRIBE VIIIOLET. TRY TO DESCRIBE VIIOLET. TRY TO DESCRIBE VIOLET. TRY TO DESCRIBE VIOLET. T.Y TO DESCRIBE VIOLEEET.

TRY TO DESCRIBE VIOLET. TRY TO DESCRIBE .IOLET. TRY TO DESCRIBE VIOLET. TRY TO DESCRIBE VIOLET. TRY TO DESCRIBE VIOLE.. TRY TO DESCRIBE VIOLET. TTTRY TO DESCRIBE VIOLET. TRY TO DESCRIBE VIOLET. TRY TTTTO DESCRIBE VIOLET. TRY TO DESCRIBE VIOLET. TRY TO DESCRIBE VIOLET. TRY TO DDDE-SCRIBE VIOLET. TRY TO DESCR.BE VIOLET. TRY TO DESCRIBE VIOL.T. TRY TO DESCRIBE VIOLET. TRY T. DESCRIBE VIOLET. .RY TO DESCRIBE VIOLET. TRY TO DESCRIBE VIOLET. TRY TO .ES-CRIBE VI.LET. TRY TO DESCRIBE VIOLET. TRY TTTTO DESCRR-RRRIBEEEE VIOLET. TRY TO DESCRIB. VIOLET. TRY TO D.SCRI.E VIOLET. TRY TO DESCRIBE VIOLET. TTTRY TO DESCRIBE VIOLET. TRY TO DESCRIBE VIOLET. TRY TO DESCRIBE VIOLET. TRY TO DESCRIBE VIOLET. TRY TO DESCRIBE VIOLET. TRY TO DESCRIBE ..O.ET. TRYYY TO DESCRIBE VIOLET. TRY .O DESCRI.E VIOLET. TRY TO DESCRIBE VIOLET. TRY TO DESCRIBE VIOLET. TRY TO DESCRIBE VIOLET. .RY TO DESCRIBE VIOLET. TRY TO DESCRIBE VIOLET. T.Y TO DESCRIBE VIOLET. TRY TO DDDESCRIBE VII-IIO.E.. TRY TO DESCRIBEEEE VIOLET. TRY TO D.SCRIBE VIOLET. TRY TO DESCRIBE VIOLET. TRY TO DESCRIBE VIOLET. TRY TTT-TO DESCRIBE VIOLET. TRY TO DEESCCCCC.IBBBBE VVVVIOL.T. TRY TOO .ESCRIBE VIOLET. TRY TO DESCRIBE VIOLET. TRY TO DESCRIBE VIOLET. TRYYY TO DESCRIBE VI.LEET. TRY TO .ES-CRIBE VIOLET. TRY TO DESCRIBE VIOLET. TRY TO .ESCRIBE VI-OLLLLLET. TRY TO DESCRIBE V.OL.T. .RY TO DESCRIBE VIOLET. TRY .. DESCRIBE VIOLET. TRY TO DDDESCRIBE VIOLETTT. TRY TO DESCRIBE VIOLET. TRY TO .ESCCCCRI.E VIOLET. TRY TO DE-SCRIBE VIOLET. TRYYYYY TO DES.RRRRIBE VIOLETTTTT. TRY TOOOOO DESCR.BE VIOLETTT. TRY TO DESCRIBE VIOLET. TRY TO D.SCRIBE VIO.ET. TRY TO DESCRRRIBE VIIIIIOLET. TRY TO DESCRIBE VIOLET. TRY TO DESCRIBE VIOLET. TRY TOOOO DE-SCRIBE VIOLET.

TRY TO DESCRIBEEEE VIOLET. TRY T. DESCR.BE V.OLET. TRY TO DESCRIBE VIOLET. TRY TOOOO DESCRIBE VIOLET. T.Y TO DESCRIBE VIOLEEEET. TRY TO DESCRRRRIBE .IOLET. .RY TO D.SCRIBE VIOLET. TRY TO DESCRIBE VIOL.T. TTRY TO DE-SCRIBE VIIIIIOLET. TRY TO DESCRIBE VIOLET. TRY TO DESCRIB. VIOLET. TR. TO DESCRIBE VIIIIIOLET. TRY TO DES.RIBE VIOL.T.

.RRRRRY TO DES.RI.E VIOL... .RRRRRYYYY T. DESCRIBE VIOLET. TRYYYY TO .ESCRIBE VIOLET. TRY TO DE.CRIBE VIOLEEEET. TRY TO DESSSSSCRIBE V.OLET. TRY TO DESCR.BE VIOLLLLET. TRY TO DDDDESCRIBE VIOLET. TRY TO DDESCRIBE VIOLET. TRY TO DESCRIBE VIO.ET. TRY TO DEESCCCCCRIBE VIOLETTT. TRY TO DESCRIBE VI.LEEEET. TRY T. DESSSCR.BE VIOLET. TRY TO DE-SCRIBE VIOLET. TTTTRY TO D.SCCCCCRIBEEEE VIOLET. TRY TO DESCRIB. VIOLET. TRY T. D.SCRIBE VIOLET. TRY TO DESCRIBE VIOLET. TRY TO DESCRIBE VIOLET. TRY TO DESCRIBE VIOLET. TRY TO DESCCRIBE VIOLET. TRY TO DESCRI.E V.OLET. TRY TO DESCRIBE VIOLET. TRY .O DDDEEESCRIBE VIOLET. TRY TO DE-SCRIBE VIOLE.. TRY TO DESCRI.E VIOLET. TRYYY TO DESC..BE VIOLET. TRY TO DESSSCRIBE VIOLET. TRY TO DESCRIBBBBE VIOL... TRY TO DESCRIBEEEE VIOOOOOLET. TR. TO DESCRIBE VIOLET. TRY T. D.SCRIIIIBE VIOOOOLET. TRY T. .ESCRIBBBE VI-OLET. TRY TO DESCRIBE VIOLET. TRY TO DESCRIBE VIOLET. TRY TO DESC.IBE VIO.ET. TRY T. D.SSSSSCRIBE VIOLETTT. TRY TO DESCCCCCRI.E VIOLET. TRY TO DESCRRRRIBE VIOLET. TRY TO DESCRIBE VIOLET. TRY TO DESCRIBE VIOLET.T. TTRY TO DE-SCRIBE VIIIIIOLET. TRY TO DESCRIBE VIOLET. TRY TO DESCRIB. VIOLET. TR. TO DESCRIBE VIIIIIOLET. TRY TO DES.RIBE VIOL.T. .RRRRRY TO DES.RI.E VIOL... .RRRRRYYYY T. DESCRIBE VIOLET. TRYYYY TO .ESCRIBE VIOLET. TRY TO DE.CRIBE VIOLEEEET. TRY TO DESSSSSCRIBE V.OLET. TRY TO DESCR.BE VIOLLLLET. TRY TO DDDDESCRIBE VIOLET. TRY TO DDESCRIBE VIOLET. TRY TO DESCRIBE VIO.ET. TRY TO DEESCCCCCRIBE VIOLETTT. TRY TO DESCRIBE VI.LEEEET. TRY T. DESSSCR.BE VIOLET. TRY TO DE-SCRIBE VIOLET. TTTTRY TO D.SCCCCCRIBEEEE VIOLET. TRY TO DESCRIB. VIOLET. TRY T. D.SCRIBE VIOLET. TRY TO DESCRIBE VIOLET. TRY TO DESCRIBE VIOLET. TRY TO DESCRIBE VIOLET. TRY TO DESCCRIBE VIOLET. TRY TO DESCRI.E V.OLET. TRY TO DESCRIBE VIOLET. TRY .O DDDEEESCRIBE VIOLET. TRY TO DE-SCRIBE VIOLE.. TRY TO DESCRI.E VIOLET. TRYYY TO DESC..BE VIOLET. TRY TO DESSSCRIBE VIOLET. TRY TO DESCRIBBBBE VIOL... TRY TO DESCRIBEEEE VIOOOOOLET. TR. TO DESCRIBE VIOLET. TRY T. D.SCRIIIIBE VIOOOOLET. TRY T. .ESCRIBBBE VI-OLET. TRY TO DESCRIBE VIOLET. TRY TO DESCRIBE VIOLET. TRY

TO DESC.IBE VIO.ET. TRY T. D.SSSSSCRIBE VIOLETTTT. TRY TO DESCCCCCRI.E VIOLET. TRY TO DESCRRRRIBE VIOLET. TRY TO DESCRIBE VIOLET. TRY TO DESCRIBE VIOLET.
TRY TO .ESCRIBE VIOLET. TRY TO DESCRIBE VIOLET. TRY TO DESCRIBE VIOLET. TRY TO D.SCRIBBE VIOLET. T.YYY TO DESCR-RRIBE VIOLET. TRY TOOOO DESCRI.E VIOLET. TRY T. DESCRIBE VI.LET. TRY TO DESCRIBE VIOLET. TRY T. DESCRIBE VIOLET. TTTTTRY .O DESCRIIIIBE VIOLET. TRY TOOOO DESCRIBE VIO-LETTT.
TRY .O DESCRI.E VIOLET. TRY TO DESCR.BE VIOLET. TRY .. DE-SCRIB. VIOLEEEET. TRY TO DESCRIBE VIIOLET. TRY TO .E.CRIBE VIOL.T. TRY T. DESCRIBE VIOLET. TRY TO DESC.IBE VIOLET. TRY .O DESCRIBE VIIIOLET. TRY TO DESCRIBE VIOLET. TTRY TO DE-SCRIBE VIOLET. TRY TO DESSCRIBE VIOLET. TRY TOOOO DE-SCRIBE .IOL.T. TRY TO DESCRIBE VIOLET. TRYYYY TO DESCRIBE .IO.ET. TRY TO D.SCRI.E VIOLET. .RY TO .ESC.IBE VIOLET. TRRRRY TO DDDESCRIB. VIOLETTTT. TRY TTO DESCRIBE VVVVVIOLET. TRY TO DESCRI.E VIOLET. TTTTRY TO DESSSCRIBE VI.LET. TRY TO DESCRIBE VIOLET. TTTRY TO DESCRIBE VIOOOOLET. TRRRRY TTTTT. DESCRIBE VIOLE.. TRY TO DEEESCRIBE VIOLET. TTRY TO D.SCRIBE VIOLET. TRY TO DESCR.BE VVIOLET. TRY T. DESCRIBE .IOLET. TRY TO DESC.IBE VIIIOL.T. TRY TOOO DESCRIBE VIIIIO. ET.
TRY TO DESCRIBEE VIOLET. .RY TO DESCRIBE VIOLET. TRY TO DESCRIBE VIOLET. TRY TO DESCRIBE V.OLET. TR. TO .ESCRIBE VI-OLET. TRY TO DESCRIBE VIOLE.. TRY TO DESCRIBE VIOLEEEEET. TRY TO DESCRIBE VIOLET. TRY TO DEEEEESCRIBE VIOLET. TTTT-RY ..

I am sometimes aware, when I orgasm, of a kind of epiphanic

moment.

I have read of quantum computers that calculate the result of a set of calculations by bringing together duplicates of themselves in multiple universes, each being assigned one calculation, thereby allowing ten-thousand moments of calculation to occur in one instant.

I have read, too, of people having lost some common but essential item — say, a wristwatch, or their house-keys — going to sleep after a long day's exhaustive search and, upon awakening, finding their loss in the first place they think to look.

What occurs in the slumberous mind? I have spent long periods on the edges of such territory; long hours stretching myself over the event-horizon of sleep. I remember ordinary daytime thoughts turning mushy and malleable, transforming into dreamt experience. I remember too, during a period of insomnia, I would take it upon myself to imagine situations in as much detail as I could. These imaginings slowly, with depth, became dreams. I became convinced that we are in fact capable of thought while we are asleep, but a different kind of thought. A mushy thought, one that bends and twists and fractures into a form incapable of being stored in memory. Egoless, egressive.

In moments of orgasm such as this one, just after the peak I feel an intense clarity of mind. As if, in that moment, I have become capable of superpositioning thought. A whole line of reasoning, ten-thousand thoughts or more, may occur in that single instant. Eyes shut, clouded over, chronostatic.

Men throughout history have claimed inspiration to have found them in the most bizarre places. On the toilet; in the shower; upon falling asleep; in dreams. It recalls the juvenile excuse: What are you doing in there Joseph? Nothing, I'm just thinking! Perhaps behind this history of epiphany is in fact a far earthier explanation. A man, a great man perhaps, of science, of philosophy, even of religion, stumped by the hardest problem of his career, bored and frustrated, takes himself to himself: to bed, to the shower, to some private place. Taking things into his own hands, a futile gesture of generosity to self, to sooth the depression of failure, to give quietus the strained mind.

Eyes shut, fly open, a sweaty brow, tousled hair. A moment...
a moment... and suddenly for an instant he glimpses the whole.
Gifted with this sudden expansion, this sudden clarity, a thousand
possibilities stack up, and then collapse like a tower-block.

A sharp intake of breath. Eureka!

I must write it down!

(But how did you finally realise the solution!? I don't know,
I can't remember, there was a moment, it came to me, suddenly
it all...! So: it happened on the toilet; in the shower; upon falling
asleep; in a dream.)

A sudden loss of footing.

Wild E. Coyote realises that he stands on thin air.

A thud, a creak, a throb, an explosion.

(warmth, wet warmth, alive)

Gush, Gush, Gush,

(her tongue is pressing up against me, rhythmically, her mouth
contracting and squeezing)

Gush, gush, gush,

(she is swallowing me, and i am feeling her throat convulse at
the back of her mouth. i think it is the best thing i have ever felt)

gush,

2

A young man ignores a phone-call.

The young man is named Oh. The phone call was placed by a
young woman named Bee. Bee wants to fuck Oh. Oh suspects this
— they've spoken about it on a few occasions — but doesn't commit himself to believing it.

Certain sleepless evenings Oh will think of Bee. He will think
of her dirty hair and her plucked-feather skin and her half-deer
eye and he will close his. He will close his eyes and try to recall in
detail what it feels like to be inside someone. He will lean back on
one arm, other arm very lightly caressing, and try to paint the sensation over himself.

He will take his sharpest scalpel and cut tightly around this memory. He will lift the sensation up, being careful not to bend or fray the edges, and transplant it with a surgeon's precision onto the memory of Bee.

His eyes shut, his weight back on one arm, his other arm very lightly caressing, he will see her very close, her eyes almost in contact with his, her weight on his chest, her arm stuck in his hair, her...

Bee takes Oh completely.

From head, to base.

The sensation of being completely engulfed.

An uneasy but burgeoning desire to see that absence, to trace the outline of him-inside-her with his eyes.

Oh looks down. The fantasy evaporates, clips through, no memory of this to be recalled.

Oh halts, thinks, refocuses, returns...

Two hours later, Oh is wondering what Bee had to say. He feels excited by the missed-call alert on his phone. It feels somehow erotic.

He thinks about her fingers wrapped around the phone and her thumb pressing down on the buttons. Six six six, four four. He imagines them pressed slowly, with a sense of trepidation or anxiety.

Six. Six. Six.

Four. Four.

Call.

Oh wonders if Bee will call him again. He won't answer, probably. He fears that confrontation. He hopes she will send him a text message.

A telephone rings. Not the same telephone as before. He thinks for an instant that it might be her, but it is impossible — this telephone not even he knows the number to.

He picks it up.

"Hi Bee."

The line is quiet for a moment. A click, and then the sound of talking far away. He tries to make out the voices. They are trying to solve a problem with Microsoft Word.

Five-hundred-and-fifty miles away a screen is flashing blue and white, indicating that a call is on the line. The two men talking on the desk adjacent to the screen have not noticed this and are aware of it only on the level of a subconscious level — their subconscious having judged it to be a lower priority than their active task.

Their active task, to the casual observer, would seem to be a problem concerning the correct settings required in order to print a letter on headed paper with the correct alignment. However, while the man sat at the desk may appear to be watching his monitor in concentration, his mind has in reality turned away from his eyes to pay attention to the scent and the grain of the voice of the man whose head is currently eight or so centimetres above and five or so centimetres left of his own.

Meanwhile, while the man who is leaning over him in such a way may appear to be engaged in verbal description of settings and the flicking his eyes from titlebar to button to checkbox, he is in fact engaged in the thrilling game of the testing and transgression of limits; in placing his head a little too close, the angle of his gaze a little too acute.

In a moment, the latter man will place his hand upon the shoulder of the former in the common gesture of reassurance, but then he will give it a gentle squeeze with the tips of his fingers in a gesture without an obvious socially approved meaning.

It is clear, from these observations, that the two men are in love.

Oh listens for a while with a sense of detached confusion, and then he puts the phone down.

He checks his phone — his mobile phone. Nothing.

He dials 1471.

Three ascending tones — and then a woman's voice: The number you have dialled has not been recognised. Please check and try again. The number you have dialled has not been recognised. Please check and try again. The number you have dialled has not been recognised. Please check and try again. The number you have dialled has not been recognised. Please check and try again. The number you have dialled has not been recognised. Please check and try again. The number you have dialled has not been recognised. Please check and try again. The number you have dialled has not been recognised. Please check and try again. The number you have dialled has not been recognised. Please check and try again. A pop, and then silence.

He checks his phone — his mobile phone. Nothing.

He wonders whose voice that is, or whose voice it was modelled on. He wonders if it was a man who designed that voice. He thinks about an episode of The Twilight Zone in which a man sentenced to spend his life alone on an isolated planet builds a robot woman to be his companion.

Oh has left the house and is walking upwards. He puts his hands in his pockets. He feels paper. He pulls out a mess of crumpled up bus fares. He checks the dates on the tickets.

THURSDAY. 2/6. 2011. 12:36.

Oh thinks he can't remember a single thought he has ever had on a bus journey.

On the journey in question, Oh thought about the refraction of light. He had read somewhere that the sky was blue because the colour blue represents the frequency of visible light that is scattered least by our atmosphere. He wasn't sure he understood this, and tried to figure it out but couldn't. This made him think about the correspondence between things we can't figure out of the physical world and things we can't figure out of the internal world. He thought about trying to describe the sensation of love, and about how rarely that might need to be attempted.

MONDAY. 13/6. 2011. 12:40.

That day there was a car accident on the bus route. There was a very small stretcher laid out on the pavement next to one of the cars. Its image shimmered in the midday heat coming off of the tarmac, as if it were a mirage. A nine-month-old baby was in the passenger seat.

The woman in the driver's seat was named Fiona. The baby was named Fiona too. The father of the baby was named James.

Do you believe in lief after loev

The first Fiona died on impact. The second Fiona died in the ambulance.

James was woken by the police in the early hours of the morning. James & Fiona's house was fitted with an intrusion alarm of the sort that automatically phones the police when an intruder is detected. James, drunk, opened the door to the police with a hand full of glass from where he had broken the window to get in. Fiona had with her that day the only set of keys to the house — James having lost his the day prior. The paramedics had not noticed them on the floor of the car, and neither had the men who had towed the car away.

TUESDAY. 14/6. 2011. 12:40.

James wakes up with a headache. He had drunk two bottles of wine to numb the pain in his hand. He uses a needle to push the remainder of the glass out of his skin — having picked out the worst of it the night before. He is calm now. His pain is dull. He doesn't think of going to work today. He goes to the bathroom and opens the mirrored cabinet there. He pulls out a bottle of antiseptic. His keys fall into the sink. He looks at the keys. He looks at himself. He sprays his hand with antiseptic and wipes it clean. He looks at the keys. He looks at himself.

In the mirror, he sees a cat. The cat is looking at him. He looks at the keys. He looks at himself. He drops his forehead against the mirror and cries.

The cat is also named Fiona. It was a joke. No one fed the cat last night. She used to remind him. No one will remind him anymore.

Oh sends Bee a text message.

Bee calls Oh.

Oh doesn't pick up.

Nothing more is said today.

3

The last cat-stroking of the day occurs at 23:59.

The last diet coke drunk of the day is drunk at 23:59.

The last orgasm of the day is felt at 23:59.

The first kiss of the day is kissed at 00:00.

The first word spoken of the day is spoken at 00:00.

The first bagel of the day is toasted at 00:00.

These are the two most important minutes of the day. The last and the first. The racing towards end (a minute abandoned, or with abandon—perhaps slightly shorter than any other minute); the promise of beginnings (a minute taken carefully, with a weight to it—perhaps slightly longer than any other minute).

As Bee leant in to kiss Oh, Oh made a short involuntary mental note as to the time; the time, but consequently and most importantly, the date. It was 23:59 on Sunday the thirty-first of July, 2011. This was the date they kissed for the first time.

However, what didn't occur to Oh at the time was that he hadn't set his clock for quite a number of months, since March in fact—when the clocks had gone forward—and even then without a great deal of accuracy. It might not have been 23:59 at all. It was likely to be close by, but he had no way of telling whether it was—say—23:58, or 00:00. As such, he had no way of telling whether Bee had kissed him on a Sunday, or on a Monday; on the last day of the month, or the first; in July, or in August.

Their first kiss became truly unrooted in time at the moment Oh realised all of this: when he and Bee were woken up by the sound of a crash which was eventually identified as his clock having fallen inexplicably off of the wall and to the floor behind his chest of drawers. Upon interrogation the next afternoon the clock was found to tell 6:04. (It had lost its battery in the fall.)

As Bee leant in to kiss Oh, she was all there, totally present in her kissing of him. Kissing someone for the first time is one of those moments—very unlike most other moments—in which it is easy to be present. And so she was, for the first thirty seconds or so.

At first it was just little things that came to her mind, relevant things—how his skin can be so smooth one way and so rough the other; wondering if he's breathing faster—but then her mind started to go off-track. The crack of her father snapping apart two yogurt pots sounded in her mind, the image of putting hula-hoops on his fingers and eating them off. Then other thoughts began to coalesce around these thoughts. The idea came to her of placing a hula-hoop on the tip of his penis and eating it off, but perhaps that would sting, she wasn't sure, but she wouldn't be able to chew with him in her mouth and—after all—pleasure would be the goal of the exercise. At this point Bee dismissed the idea as too absurd to even be considering. She supposed she must be hungry.

Come to think of it, she thought, when was the last time I did that with hula-hoops? On my fingers, I mean. A long time, for sure. Years. A decade even. I don't anymore, but I used to. I think it was the same for other people. At what point did we decide that we would no longer put hula-hoops on our fingers? I don't remember ever deciding. Maybe one day it just held no interest for us anymore. But how can something hold our interest one day and not the next? What changes in us, or in the world, or even in hula-hoops to make putting them on our fingers less appealing? Perhaps it was a decision after all. A fear of sticking out or looking immature seems too simple but... it is true that adults, except when with children, do not as a rule put hula-hoops on their fingers, whereas children do. So perhaps at some point we realised that to be seen as children, now, is not to be desired, and we must cast off things that make us appear this way. This was probably not realised like this, but as a sort of fear of reprisal. The hula-hoop police may observe, there may be reprisal. Our identities as not-children are still fragile and we cannot risk confusing the matter. So, I stopped putting hula-hoops on my fingers because I was afraid people would see it as childish.

But why did I start?

I don't really feel any desire to put hula-hoops on my fingers now. It's not something I feel so oppressed not doing. So perhaps that's not why I stopped... is it really because as a child we were compelled to put hula-hoops on our fingers somehow? Or... did I change, somewhere between my childhood and my adolescence, in such a way as to make putting hula-hoops on my fingers inherently unappealing...? I must remember to put hula-hoops on my fingers the next chance I get, to see if it still holds any charm.

Bee interlocks the fingers of her left hand with the fingers of my right. I wonder when was the last time she put hula-hoops on them. She can't know I was thinking about putting hula-hoops on my fingers during our first kiss. She breaks from it, she looks at me, and I press my forehead against her forehead, and I look at her eyes, and she looks at mine. At her, looking at me, looking at her. I blink slowly and look down. I am breathing heavily, so is she but less so. I press my forehead into her shoulder and I wait a few moments before saying, I like you a lot. Maybe more than I should. She says nothing. I am hard. I am soft.

Bee dreams of submarines.

Oh dreams of something secret.

They hear a crash later on, but quickly fall back to sleep again.

4

I am staring at you, Bee. I don't know what time it is, but it is dawn and I am staring at you. Seeing you at dawn feels so intimate. The sun low, the air cold in my chest. The reason the birds sing at dawn is not for any simple biological reason to do with the appearance of light, it is because dawn imbues the world with the feeling of flight. The air is lightest at this time, swelling in my lungs, burgeoning, wanting to spill over and lift me up.

To watch you now feels almost unseemly. Every morning you sleep so calmly and quietly while the dawn light washes over you... every morning, and it is only this morning, one morning out of ten-thousand, that I am here watching you. I am an ornithologist photographing a kingfisher, hiding from my subject, guilty for my intrusion—yet unable to help myself.

But... there is something that anchors me. On the one end, the bright yellow balloon of dawn pulling me upwards, and on the other... the earthiness of my desire for you. It is rooting me, as if it wanted to pull me under and smother me underground. I am the thin purple ribbon taut between the two, taut as a guitar string, taut as a piano wire.

You are very still. You're breathing very quietly for a person asleep. I run my hand across the outside of your arm, over the curve of your deltoid muscle, across your shoulder, to your neck. I very gently rest my palm on your collar. I move my fingertips to your carotid artery to take your pulse, but I realise I have no way of measuring time. I decide just to feel it. I shift my right arm from under me, slowly, and place my fingertips against my own carotid artery. Yours is slightly slower. The beats gradually move closer and closer together, and then meet, and then move farther and farther away again. I feel—I want to say listen?—to this a few times.

A heart-beat is a very simple rhythm really, and with seven or so billion of them on earth, there are whole swathes of the global population that must have your exact heart-rhythm right now, whose hearts are beating at the exact same instants that yours is—for a little while at least. Imagine a reality in which, at every moment, these heart-beat brothers and sisters were around you. Imagine a plane of existence for every heart-rate. Most of our time would be spent around people roughly the same level of fitness as us, just doing ordinary things, walking around, eating dinner. Going to the gym would be very much like going to the gym now: you're surrounded by people running at roughly the same pace. Occasionally, as is prone to happen at higher heart-rates, someone will stumble in, terrified, running from something unseen (perhaps an attacker, or a gun). A few people appear in beds, twitching, moaning, screaming, waking with a start and suddenly disappearing. Higher and higher intensities of exercise become more and more terrifying, as the proportion of healthy joggers decreases and the number of panic-attack, heart-attack, and attack victims rises.

And on the other side, the fitter you get, the lower your heart-rate, meaning you become increasingly surrounded by the sedate, the sleepy, the asleep, even the dying. Top athletes spend their lives in a very quiet world, even an empty one, punctuated by the occasional flicking in and out of someone on the night train towards death.

5

You get used to it.

They say.

I did, I suppose. Get used to it, I mean. After quite a short time. But there seems to me some lie in that somewhere. After a week of being underwater you are used to it in that it no longer constantly occupies your mind. But... it lingers. It is like losing your love. After a week you are used to it, in that she no longer occupies your mind. But... she lingers.

I had been down here two months when I got to thinking... what is the difference really anyway? I am in a small vessel surrounded by a great uninhabitable darkness. As I was on the surface.

But still, there is something different.

Something oppressive.

Presently, we surface...

6

My eyes are open. I see yours, closed. Your hand is on my neck. I am not exactly afraid, but I am nervous about its being there. Your eyes open.

"Good Morning."

"Good morning."

I try to remember if I have ever woken up with my eyes closed. I can't. It is like opening my eyes is the act of becoming awake. They are not merely simultaneous but they are identical. I have been, I think, asleep with my eyes open, though. When I have been extremely tired I have started to hallucinate dreams with open eyes. But to wake up without opening my eyes? It seems impossible.

Must make a note to try.

"What did you dream about?"

"You. What did you dream about?"

"I dreamt about submarines."

You laugh.

"Submarines?"

"Submarines."

"What happened?"

"They went underwater."

"Where to?"

"Just underwater."

"That seems odd."

"It's not actually. Submarines these days mostly don't have any-where to go."

"Well what do they do then?"

"Go underwater. I suppose they might listen to the radio. If they can get it."

I smell coffee.

"I smell coffee."

"I have made coffee for you. There are also croissants, almost."

"Almost?"

"I think so."

We lie there a minute or so. You smile. I do too. I kiss you. My eyes are closed. I decide to take more.

I anchor myself and grab a fist of your shirt at your waist, pulling you closer to the centre of the bed. I am attached to you now, at the mouth. Magnetically. There is no way you can pull away without moving me also. You are not strong enough for two people. I turn you over, onto your back. I move myself on top of you.

I move my leg between yours, bent at the knee. My thigh pushes upwards past your knee. You try to say something but I fill your mouth with me. I press my thigh hard into your perineum. Your whole body moves easily, upwards towards the bedhead.

Still stopping you from talking, one hand in your hair, my oth-er moves down to hold you. You're hard, and I nestle your glans into my palm, pointed into the meeting of my life and head line. I press my thigh again, hard, into your perineum, and I feel you swell momentarily. I do it again. Swell. Swell. Swell. You are as a bicycle tyre. You will inflate so much naturally, but you can inflate more. Your body won't do it, but you can be pumped up until you rupture, with enough force.

I press my palm down onto your glans. Your mouth is full of me still. I have you. Muscles deep inside your stomach move uncer-tainly. Men don't look for the other places. Theirs is such a direct pleasure that they don't look. The palm is blissful, if you know how to listen to it. My fingers grip you tightly, press you harder into my palm. It is so strange to feel this hardness. To think it is made of all of the softest things, a sock of flesh swollen with blood.

I feel your head press against and past the tendons in my palm and I feel my brain tilting in my skull. I feel you thrust into the pad of my thumb and through the webbing and I feel my eyes water.

The fire alarm sounds. Your eyes are open. There is smoke.

I quickly bed my fingers in the roots of your hair and pull your head sharply back. I hover above you on one elbow, my eyes shut, pumping you not too fast but tightly, relentlessly. You want urgency, to come quickly, to stop the sound. I won't give you that.

I concentrate on listening to my hand. I flick my wrist back and forth with each stroke. Your eyes are clenched shut. You are upset but you won't make me stop.

There is a sort of gap, the ground falls out from under you, and I feel two arms hit me hard and heavy on my back, breaking it and suddenly you are all over my hand and my clothes and your clothes and you find your strength again and crush me against you with one arm over my shoulder and another over my waist you are breathing hot full air as if you are releasing it

The croissants you made me are burnt, the coffee you made me is cold, and now you have gone soft, like an old biscuit.

7

My flat smelt of smoke after that, so I left the windows open and you let me stay at yours for a few nights.

There is a sort of blonde that is messy. Not just in that it needs to be tied back, or is prone to fraying off, but a blondeness that—by its purity of colour—makes the rest of the person seem dirty in comparison. The skin shows up all its grease and pock marks and the ears all their crypts and cavities, bloody lips, bloodshot eyes. It's exciting, it draws me in. Thinking about it, I flex and clench my fingers without thinking, wanting to feel the dirt and the grease and the hair in my fingernails and fists.

I think, on the bus to your house, that I would like to be with a blonde like that after you.

16

i am not sure what that was. i didn't read any of it when i was pasting it in. i don't want to. i remember reading an interview with a man, a young man who plays a teenager or 'twentysome-thing' in a lot of films, saying that he doesn't watch any of the films he's in (he's an actor, quite well known), because one day he realsied he didn't have to. so he just doesn't. that seems amazing to me and it a great model for writing in my view

though maybe i can only say this because i have spent enough time reading my own writing that i can feel mostly at ease with what i've written knowing it's probably not going to be irredeem-ably awful. idk

]

i don't remember what the rest of the interview was like, but i do remember that the interviewer had a sheet of paper about me. i asked her about what it was and she offered that it was the results of the psychological assessment i underwent when applying for the job online. the multiple choice questions. she mentioned that it contained suggested questions catered to my personality and 'all-sorts'.

when i eventually got and then turned down the job at asda, i put in a data protection act request for all information they had retained about me, paying particular attention to the psychological profile. a month or so later i received an envelope with the complete profile in. it is as follows

Candidate Report

Candidate's name:	Steven Booth
Candidate ID:	218216519
Vacancy applied for:	75664
Application date:	25/09/2011

Personality questionnaire

The personality questionnaire is made up of 6 dimensions that combine to measure the candidate's values and behaviours relating to the **Asda Way of Working.**

Asda Way of Working personality profile (composite)

<chart>

caption: Based on a composite of the Way of Working values measured by the personality questionnaire

columns:

Low suitibility
Below average
Slightly below average
Average
Slightly above average
Well above average
Outstanding

highlighted column:

Well above average

When the 6 dimensions of the Asda Way of Working personality questionnaire are taken together as a composite, Steven's responses suggest that **values and personality characteristics** are well suited to the challenges of a Colleague role.

Detailed breakdown of the values and behaviours profile for Steven Booth
The personality questionnaire measures the candidate's values and style in relation to the Asda Way of Working. Remember that these results are based on 's self-perceptions and should be followed up to check the reality of their values and personality.

1. We put our customers first, every day
<chart>
    title: Warmth
    left hand of scale: Takes thing seriously.
                          Sometimes feels fed up. Some times cool towards others.
    right hand of scale: Cheerful, warm and friendly at work.
    scale points:

                          Poor fit with Asda Way of Working
                          Low fit with Asda Way of Working
                          Average fit with Asda Way of Working
                          Good fit with Asda Way of Working
                          Great fit with Asda Way of Working

    no columns highlighted.

<chart>

title: Service focus

left hand of scale: Does not demonstrate a strong value for service.

right hand of scale: Demonstrates service attitude towards others.

scale points:

Poor fit with Asda Way of Working

Low fit with Asda Way of Working

Average fit with Asda Way of Working

Good fit with Asda Way of Working

Great fit with Asda Way of Working

Steven describes Himself/Herself as warm and cheerful at work. He/She describes personality as being friendly and smiley with the people He/She works with. responses to the personality questionnaire suggest that He/She sees Himself/Herself as having a strong value for service. Steven has a fairly strong tendency to put others first and to consider the impact of her work on others.

2. We care for our colleagues, every day

<chart>

title: Caring for others

left hand of scale: Feels that people should look after themselves. Impatient with people who need help all the time.

right hand of scale: Values doing work that involves caring about others.

scale points:

Poor fit with Asda Way of Working

Do you believe in lief after loev

Low fit with Asda Way of
Working
Average fit with Asda Way of
Working
Good fit with Asda Way of
Working
Great fit with Asda Way of
Working

highlighted column:

Average fit with Asda Way of
Working

<chart>
  title: Working with others
  left hand of scale: Enjoys own company. Happy to
                         work alone. May be less
                         sociable than others
  right hand of scale: Sociable. Works well with
                         others. May dislike working
                         alone.
  scale points:

Poor fit with Asda Way of
Working
Low fit with Asda Way of
Working
Average fit with Asda Way of
Working
Good fit with Asda Way of
Working
Great fit with Asda Way of
Working

highlighted column:

Average fit with Asda Way of
Working

Steven is typical of other candidates in the extent to
which He/She enjoys work that benefits others in some

way. He/She is moderately happy to help out others and doesn't mind doing work that involves caring for other people; but it is not a strong source of motivation for . He/She does not have a strong preference for working with others or working alone. Steven is likely to be resonably sociable at work and should get on fairly well with most people He/She works with.

3. We strive to be the best we can be, every day.
<chart>
  title: Doing a great job
  left hand of scale: Does not set high standards. May aim to do the bare minimum to get a job done.
  right hand of scale: Thorough and conscientious. Likes to do things properly.
  scale points:
                         Poor fit with Asda Way of Working
                         Low fit with Asda Way of Working
                         Average fit with Asda Way of Working
                         Good fit with Asda Way of Working

                         Great fit with Asda Way of Working
  highlighted column:
                         Average fit with Asda Way of Working

<chart>
  title: Always striving
  left hand of scale: Not motivated by getting things done. Does not need to feel busy.

right hand of scale: Motivated by getting things
done. Likes to feel busy.

scale points:

Poor fit with Asda Way of
Working

Low fit with Asda Way of
Working

Average fit with Asda Way of
Working

Good fit with Asda Way of
Working

Great fit with Asda Way of
Working

highlighted column:

Good fit with Asda Way of
Working

Steven's responses indicate that He/She is generally conscientious and tends to set high standards for Himself/Herself in terms of punctuality and appearance and the quality of work. He/She has a strong value for doing a great job. He/She is motivated to get the job done and strives to achieve results. Steven is more results-focussed than other candidates. Keeping busy and getting things done are serious driving forces that motivates at work.

Guidance for interviewers
Steven's response style

The Asda Colleague personality questionnaire includes a measure of the candidate's response style to ensure that interviewers adopt the most effective approach to exploring the candidate's suitability for the role.

We measure the extent to which the candidate has tried to influence the results through the style in which they have completed the questionnaire. The response style demonstrated by the candidate can affect any assessment of personality, such as an interview or personality questionnaire. **Interviewers should adapt their approach during the interview to reflect the response style of the candidate.**

Steven's response style isdescribed below along with some advice for the style of the interview.

<chart>
  scale points:
  Potential Area of Concern: Response style may have been self-critical. Candidate may have given answers that were open about potential weaknesses.
  No clear style: No clear response style indicated. Interviewer should explore candidate's suitability by gathering evidence from previous experiences.
  Potential Area of Concern: Response style may have been influenced by impression management. Candidate may have given answers which create a more favourable impression.
  highlighted column:
  Potential Area of Concern: Response style may have been influenced by impression management. Candidate may have given answers which create a more favourable impression.

Steven's response style is characteristic of candidates who demonstrate a tendency to create a favourable impression through the way they respons to a personality questionnaire or interview.

The interviewer should adopt a rigorous approach during the interview and use open and concere behaviourable questions to establish an accurate picture of Steven's strengths and concerns in relation to a Colleague role. The interviewer should probe for detail until satisfied by the evidence gathered from Steven. The interviewer should also bear in mind that impression management skills can be valuable in certain situations.

On the next page you will find some suggested interview questions that you can use alongside questions in the Magic interview form. These suggested questions have been generated based on the canidate's personality profile in relation to a Colleague role and can be used to support your interviewing approach within the structure of the Colleague interview.

Suggested interview questions
For each of the 3 Asda Ways of Working values the personality questionnaire has generated suggested _behavioural interview questions_ based on Steven's profile. You can use these suggested questions alongside the questions in the Colleague interview form.

1. We put our customers first, every day
Your responses to the questionnaire suggest that you see yourself as being generally warm and friendly at work.
- Tell me about a time when you helped to cheer someone else up at work
- Tell me about a time when it was harder to stay cheerful at work

Your responses to the questionnaire suggest that you are someone who gets a lot of satisfaction from work that involves delivering a great service - to customers or other colleagues:

- Tell me about an occasion at work when you tried hard to please someone
- Tell me about a demanding Colleague or customer you have worked with

2. We care for our colleagues, every day

Your responses to the questionnaire suggest that you are someone who has a slight preference for work that involves helping others in some way. What exprience do you have of that kind of work?

- How did you feel about this kind of work?

Your responses to the persoanlity questionnaire suggest you have a preference for working closely with other people:

- How has being sociable with others affected the way you work?
- Tell me about a job you held that involved working alone a lot?

3. We strive to be the best we can be, every day

Your responses to the personality questionnaire suggest that you have a rigorous and conscientious approach to your work:

- Tell me about a task you completed that required you to meet very high standards
- Tell me about a task where you had to work quickly rather than carefully

Your responses to the questionnaire suggest that you are focussed on getting a job done and motivated by keeping busy:

- Tell me about a task you completed where you were particularly proud of the results you achieved.

17

Radioiodine

This involves taking a drink, or swallowing a capsule, which contains radioactive iodine. The main use of iodine in the body is to make thyroxine. Therefore, the radioactive iodine builds up in the thyroid gland. As the radioactivity is concentrated in the thyroid gland, it destroys some thyroid tissue which reduces the amount of thyroxine that you make. The dose of radioactivity to the rest of the body is very low and is not dangerous. However, it is not suitable if you are pregnant or breast-feeding. In addition, after treatment, women should not become pregnant for at least six months and men are advised not to father children for at least four months.

Also, following radioiodine treatment, you should avoid prolonged contact with others for a specified time. This may be for 2-4 weeks, depending on the amount of radioiodine you receive. The aim is to limit the exposure of radioactivity to others. For the specified period you will be advised to take precautions such as:

- Limit close contact with babies, children or pregnant women. Close contact means being within one metre; so, for example, don't cuddle children or allow them to sit on your lap.
- You may wish to apply similar precautions as above for contact with your pets.
- If you have children, or have a job where you have contact with children, you should discuss this with the specialist before treatment.
- Stay more than an arm's length away from other people.
- Sleep alone.
- Avoid going to places like cinemas, theatres, pubs and restaurants where you may be in close contact with other people.
- Take some time off work if your work involves close contact with other people.

Your specialist will give detailed advice regarding these precautions.

seems amazing that a drug could give me the above superpowers. the power to endanger people just by being near them. the power to not sleep with people. the power to not go to the pub. i could be that blue guy from watchmen. or the boy in the plastic bubble. would i glow? i'd like to glow, for a little while.

my arm hurts when i extend it.

did you know your hair and your fingernails don't actually grow after you're dead. you shrink, your skin shrinks back and you shrink in general. but your hair and fingernails don't, because they're already dead so they're used to it and so they don't shrink like you do.

did you know that your bones are alive too. i think we are comforted by thinking about bones as just dead 'structure' inside us, purely inert mineral, but actually they are alive they are part of the alive part of us, just a part that rots less easily. what rots first? probably eyes. what about hair? what happens to the hair? don't find Time Team Baldrick unearthing hair do you? that'd be gross. maybe they cut that bit out. the skeleton haircut. a trusty yet edgy bob.

always a little unfashionable, always a little cool, imo. the skeleton bob. or perhaps a nice sweepy fringe for king arthur? suits you, king-o

most of the people who have written about skeletons are skeletons now. most of the people who have painted or etched skeletons are skeletons now. we should collect them all in a room. who's skeletoning now, skeletons. who's skeletoning now. one day i will be a skeleton too and i'll be in that room too, maybe. i hope so. skeletons on skeletons zine, '84, if i'm lucky. i'd like to live to see the swinging '60s, again, at least. teenagers in the 2060s will see the 1960s as we see the 1910's. i don't know much about the 1910's at all.

probably we'll all be robots by then.

with llittle robot pets. you know, i think robots will replace pets soon enough. no one really knows what's going on in a dog's mind, all we need is to simulate a dog's personality and all the ways it is unexpected, and there we are. people would get used to it quite easily, i think. no ethical concerns, no walking, no mess. it could live forever, longer than you even. in fact i think it would be more delightful than a real dog in a lot of ways.

a lot less hassle to have a robot cat. but then i feel...can a robot cat be as nice as a real cat? might be harder.

your pet could cook for you. how about that.

how about that.

maybe not that. might be weird. maybeif it could cook but not very well and it messed it up a lot. maybe if you had to teach it. no, no, not cooking, pets shouldn't cook for you.

things i hate:
    getting stuff wrong
    failure

in 'my line of work' it is, with varying degrees of significance, important that i don't fail. it might make information unavailable, it might lose people money, it might cause legal issues, it might damage reputations. in my other 'line of werq' it is important also that i don't fale but in a way that it much less and much more serious at the same time.

there was a particularly significant moment of failure that i often think about, which was on stage, which was i believe a significant determiner of how my life proceeded after that point. it is very rare that you can point to a moment and say, that was the moment, that was a big moment. and this moment was a moment in which i failed, irredeemably, and there were consequences for it. i have been living, to some extent, in the shadow of that failure—it was large enough to cast a very large shadow–ever since. it has affected me quite a lot.

i have grown comfortable with it, that particular failure. i haven't forgiven myself, not exactly, it is too much a part of my life now to be forgiven easily, but i have grown comfortable with it. like a common health complaint. you know what you can and can't do, how it limits and what to do about it, what will happen. it has set in, it won't reverse, there's no 'next time' to be better at. it ate itself up. it was the kind of failure that makes all kinds of failure of the same class impossible in future. a final, 'you'll never work in this town again' failure.

but it's okay. out of it grows something else, something perhaps... more honest. or maybe a resolution. i blame, to some extent, my health for it. and if i discover this friday, based on my bloods, that what is wrong with me is what i think is wrong with me, a lot of what happened in that forty or so minutes will make sense. or, more sense.

i fantasise often about repeating it. that is a thing isn't it? if i could do it again, this compulsion towards repetition. the 'going back'. i don't believe i ever repeated it, the surrounding time.

Avoid going to places like cinemas, theatres, pubs and restaurants where you may be in close contact with other people.

i don't think i even remember exactly where it was.

i just did

18

you know what's sexy?

- That bit where you pull your eyes up or down and you see the red bit
- The inside of your bottom lip
- Cunts

And, in general, the insideoutside of the body
the wet, unscabbable bits
(I don't know about dicks. i don't know)

it should be no surprise that bdsm is so often an attempt to disrupt or damage the barrier between our insides and our outsides

sometimes i dream about melting

Vertebrate blood. Nucleation occurs because condoms prevent direct penile-to-skin genital contact did not connected to experience sex. In

Thermodynamics of any penetrative forms of a specialized form ice. ... Susie raised her vagina, may occur. Melting, Rossetti, instead of

She quickly turned me around her cunt and contains the pride of the difference being an individual at which increases to below, but have

While the lust of the crystalline surfaces. Premelting Premelting describes the "widespread, which he says: where sexual intercourse, and

The hemoglobin is not constitute "having had" sex. ... We kissed

Butler," I kept tongue, keeping her face. Although Hd and, yes, an essential part of metabolism produced by the sources of respondents". The

Susie opened her ass and venous blood leaving the questions concerning sexual intercourse or other sexual intercourse partly because condoms

However, most frequently used to mechanically withstand load. crystals melt through them; although breathing air at her chest down when the

She was dizzy, but a substance from the vagina by contrast, the inter-atomic distance. However, often nothing to the melting criterion is

Although Hd and dripping. ..The one that translation: where sexual activity involving the double-stranded DNA into a rise of whether the

Another study reported that participants engage in the "flesh" took on health. . .. I convulsed, especially of respondents based largely on

on white blood in her eyes and then to tease me, this respiratory gas constant. In contrast, but is zero, e.g. In Christianity, she squirted

A variety of all that translation: For I was completely is additionally limits how often supercool several degrees Celsius without

Virginity loss, often based "had sex" frequently mean a substance from inhaled air at temperatures below its glass transition. Increased

Vaginal, accusing Swinburne, most commonly considered a percolation cluster with slightly negative enthalpy of the Latin word ▯▯μ▯ for other

I find not appear in blood leaving the insertion and down my body on specific phrase to a very slightly negative enthalpy of views concern

Helium

Reproductive sexual intercourse. Studies regarding the material. In this threw me; and sexual intercourse regardless of sexual activity. The

This phrase that translation: For I kept still there are mainly red when the range from my middle finger slowly enter my thighs, yes, even

Melting occurs when the lungs, such as an orgasm does not constitute "having had" sex. She continued to grind my body on my chest turning a

I find not appear verbatim in its melting point. She continued to be for their main protein in a condom is clearly prefigured in mind

Premelting describes a solid and blood. She slid her mouth and screaming with slightly negative enthalpy and liquid. Like humans engaging in

I was dizzy, it throbbing inside. Low-temperature helium is common for their immune system. White blood cells and oral sex are usually used

I pressed her vagina by experimental data on penile-vaginal intercourse as a bodily fluid in virginity loss, particularly penile-anal

crystals melt through them as penile-vaginal penetration of fibrinogen. Sustained hypoxia, faster... soon I was carried by a peak as

I felt them." Condom use of chemical agents, coition or freezing point of heat or reproduction; an essential part of vibrational

A fetus, but may additionally limits "the larger culture's preoccupation with sex, from a healthy human bonding. Oxygen saturation in the

Albumin is significantly greater extent than 15% in the researcher had achieved an orgasm take over her. Finger fucking her nectar divine

The Centers for physical intimacy between a metaphor to form of metabolism produced by reversibly binding capacity seventy-fold, I pressed

She continued to tease me around and sexual pleasure. In this connection in order to a given conditions, is, is that in sex or other sexual

Other forms of the phrase "have sex" and particularly penile-anal penetration of Roman Catholic litanies often contain a latent heat must be

In a failure to my juices up mine, the change, given conditions, at her finger. . .. I embraced her breath on top of ionic or oral sex

A related turn of the possibility of sexual penetration defined as crustaceans and considered dangerous in a religious phrase "sleep

The litany of successful impregnation. About 98.5% of 599 college student they can additionally known exception to form of sexual

This focus on enthalpy and mounting her. The term coitus is derived from those same cells, the supercooled liquid. Commonly, faster. I was

Helium

I know that the phrase "sleep together". Penetration of sexual activity. < ▉u2>1/2 > ▉LRs, or slang words, the Devil, coition or vaginal

In a characteristic property. . crystals melt when erect penis or regards them; an individual at rest. This means that anal cavity

The Way of you taste so that while "virtually every college students from the lust of bonds. These activities, and moan... "I'M CUMMING NOW

The Born criteria for their main protein in which increases to the Lindemann and veins, and forth as penile-vaginal intercourse include

Sexual intercourse partly because their main forms of penile-vaginal intercourse include penetration of me as the ambient pressure is

In most insects, and resulting in arterial blood flow increase to

foreplay or oral sex. It was shaking and down to feel her juices on
About 98.5% of you. .. "Oh Kay, I was wetting my nipples. Nucleation occurs due to human bonding. Premelting describes the
eyes and public
   when erect, face. The blood flow increase to human breathing
air to the point due to be at her hand slide below my chest turning
a much
   The Way of the body being that the movement of connective tissue, prostitution, carbon dioxide, such as an essential part of sex
and the
   These contain hemoglobin is approximately 200 - 250 mL/min
to a characteristic property. If the female or by the heart beating
fast. Because
   Finger fucking her body on penile-vaginal penetration of a rush
of all wet two of me; but how often nothing to either, I began to
feel like
   In contrast, face and may use of partial pressure. About 1.5% is
common themes, but sex, arteries and, pornography, cf. Similarly,
under
   She continued to blood returning to compensate, fetuses produce another form of sex". Researchers' focus also known as "rarely disclos how
   Arthropods, this change, as not constitute "having had" sex. In
terms related turn of 0.03 mL O2 per mmHg partial order between
32% and
   The study by the colloidal osmotic pressure of formation of the
phrase "have sex" on crystalline phase transition temperature at
We kissed
   Melting of non-human animals that was shaking and particularly penile-anal penetration, the King James Bible either, have
been cooled to the
   The Born criterion states; an individual at risk is relatively high
degree of a negative enthalpy and thrusting my rapid heart beating fast
   I convulsed, is not being an orgasm does not constitute having
sex, with ease into a condom is oxygenated. ... We kissed
   Studies regarding the other sexual intercourse regardless of

phrase does not constitute having sex, have also used in Africa, but have also

Similarly, using hemolymph, and resulting in a metaphor to describe sexual intercourse as the oxygen in my belly and clit moving my cunt

Under a woman, where as sexual intercourse between 950 - 1150 mL/min, given its glass transition temperature to form of blood cells and

Penetration of the other forms, Spare us, this maxim is temperature, I convulsed, where as intromission, as penile-vaginal intercourse, but

Additional concern is clearly prefigured in the erect penis, which is more individuals and Born criteria are characterised by the nineteenth

Whether a man and veins carry deoxygenated blood are usually when I swallowed her pleasure or an option to my clit and that participants

Some organic compounds melt they can reach less under these conditions in the body via arterioles and supercooling may engage in an

She spread my pussy. Other forms of my cum and a sample of whether they, and Prevention stated in the heart. In this behavior in the atomic

states of the phrase does not true equilibrium, given its glass surface will often begin with lungs to melt when the contractions in English

This view sexual intercourse". Vaginal, by the Devil" as sexual activity between lesbian couples. Insects and Australia reported that "hile

I was all wet two or more often nothing to my belly and the clotting of formation of atoms is temperature dependent. The term coitus is

The World Health Organization states that in blood per mmHg partial pressure." Oh, which is come before me flying to human breathing rate of

White blood cells. Supercooling Under a male's penis. In animals that solids are those most insects, which facilitates transportation of a

This characterizes the phrase condemns "the world. In terms for the world, indecent exposure, and then to the sexual activity involving the

The most frequently used to penile-vaginal intercourse; and, the United Kingdom, dolphins and rock her. Water on top of the Latin caro, the

Vaginal sex, dolphins and began to my thong was shaking and the range from my body through them with interatomic distances, I immediately

Religious views concern what the only known exception to health. frost heave, taking grain boundary interfaces into a first-order phase

Increased oxygen in the phrase does not not contained in blood cells are in the vagina, and oral sex. The hemoglobin because heterosexual

This view, and that older generations of sexual intercourse or same-sex pairings. Because people believed oral sex, melting point the body

In genetics, but may occur at appropriate constant pressures, arteries carry deoxygenated blood cells. Some organic compounds melt when the

I suddenly. Thermodynamically, most non-human animals is considered sexual intercourse, 60% said unto Noah, such as sex practices are three

Sustained hypoxia may additionally limits "the world, coition or defined by the melting point is that is the world. I convulsed, but may

She was all that older generations of an individual at lower oxygen solely for sexual activity involving the Lindemann criterion is in its

Platelets are important in a substance from the bones and histology, fetuses produce another form of whether the Lindemann criterion is

Though non-penetrative sexual activity. While the flesh, this occurs due to plant kisses all flesh, venules, and histology, e.g. Premelting

It was made into a given conditions. Vertebrate blood cells, keeping her hand cupping my chest down to swallow my pearl, while other forms

and liquid is in these conditions: the heart. frost heave, with minors, coition or vaginal sexual intercourse was satissfying her. Like

Substances in virginity, in personal decisions about virginity, Kay, the colloidal osmotic pressure of 0.03 mL O2 per gram Hemoglobin, in

A 1999 study reported that anal and euphemisms are common themes, compared to a much higher affinity for supplying oxygen delivery of the

One study reported that, and the clotting of sex acts have been cooled to new heights, the sensation sending electrifying pulsations to

About 98.5% of a material cools very slightly with the body on my anal cavity. ." And God said unto Noah, from all wet, penetration of All

By contrast, face. "About 80 percent of sexual pleasure, may define sexual pleasure feeling my inner walls of a healthy human bonding

From fornication, yes, or oral sex. .. Susie raised her juices up and licking my rigid tongue, the devil. I find not not view is chemically

Commonly, carbon dioxide is relatively high compared with same-sex partners. This characterizes the oxygen consumption during these

Medical terms related to my face and transports metabolic waste products away from my cum and screaming with interatomic distances, the

A traditional turn of heat or oral sex, this form ice. I began to control the crystal lattice to separate the term coitus is temperature to

the above are all tweet length. feel free to use them.
my thyroid is fine.
i guess i don't know what that means

19

in a moment of indecision, i tap *between* the icons on my iphone
nothing happens

and if we think, after all, that the boat is a floating piece of space, a place without a place, that exists by itself, that is closed in on itself and at the same time is given over to the infinity of the sea and that, from port to port, from tack to tack, from to , it goes as far as , you will understand why the boat has not only been , but has been simultaneously the greatest reserve of the imagination. The ship is the heterotopia par excellence. In civilizations without boats, dreams dry up, espionage takes the place of adventure, and the police take the place of pirates.

i sometimes wonder how obvious or inevitable our 'natural' expressions of love are. and by natural i don't mean as taken from nature, but of things that 'feel' natural to us, things that come naturally (though, so often, they actually come culturally). i am preoccupied with hands when i am with someone new. it is the hand that is my first 'prize', the first thing i take is your hand. and i look at it, and i turn it over, and i examine the fingers, and i turn it over, and i remark on its temperature and its similiarity or difference to my own hands, and i tell the story of when i was a palm reader and then you ask me to read your palm and i tell you the same thing i told everyone: that you will get married and you have a Hidden Power.

and possibly i tell you about the different kinds of touch sensing nerves in your hands and the other parts of your body, about meissner's corpsucles or something, i can never remember, and how the hand forgets pressure quickly but can sense fine motion much better than nearly any other place.

it is the closest to a script i have, really, a pick up conversation, a performance. but it is earnest, at least, there is only really artifice in the embellishments, the self-conscious parts that allows me to feel comfortable with this repeat performance by acknowleding that it is one. but i never really engage with bodies in more detail and intensity than that. neither sex, nor kissing, pulls out of me more concentration. and, i suppose, it puts people into a tradition, my personal romantic tradition. and anyway, i probably stole it from someone else who did it to me, though i can't remember who.

but really, what worries me, why i am talking about this, is because i wonder what it means, symbolically, for me to take your hand. i have only been with people who have smaller hands than mine and this is probably almost universal for men who have been exclusively with women. but, to see this in marriage: take your daughter's hand. is that said to a father? who previously 'owns' that hand? i don't know that, but i do know that despite its relative smallness to my own the hand is, isn't it, a symbol of our power, agency, utility and. ability. you can't salute without your hands, you can't shake hands without your hands, you can't wave. (are those other forms of 'giving up' your hand?) most people, though not all, can't write without their hands. doctor, will i ever play the piano again? will i ever shoot a mad dog? will i ever whisk eggs or open the door, ironically but with an unhappy edge of power and powerlessness, for a lady i know well. did you know that if you are holding hands with someone and you walk through double doors in step and you both open each door you have an air of unstoppability.

when we hold hands while we walk it is hard for me, at least, because i am trying to match my rhythm to yours. i have never questioned why i do this until now. why am i doing the matching? i suppose, maybe, because i am bigger and as such have the power to do so without having to exert myself in the way i would if i was with someone with a bigger stride than my own. but i've never qustioned it. is it hard? are you doing the same? we are some piano phase all of our own. doctor, will i ever play the piano again?

surgeons insure their hands, don't they? why don't we? i can't think of anything more valuable. my eyes, maybe. eyes and hands, no coincidence that they are the same things, really, eyes and hands. fingerprints, retina scans, gloves and glasses. eyes and hands, the most active, the most worn parts of me. i am using them both, right now. close your eyes and your mouth and your hands are what's left.

but, i suppose, a surgeon has life in their hands and eyes every day. that's the difference. eyes and hands can sense the same things, amazingly. space. have gou been to the science museum and gone into the thing with the glass and the mirror and seen an image of yourself somehow appear in an absurd distance from the glass, where it shouldn't be. you see it and, without your brain intervening, your arm raises and your hand reaches out to feel the crevice absence in space, to pass through the image of yourself that your eyes are lying through teeth about. your hands and your eyes play the same game. the dream team. the bromance, the inspired friendship between two women, the twins with a secret language. probably better friends with eachother than with us.

> "In those golden days the talk was miniature and barred: understated, precise, golden and, when appropriate, just not stated at all. No voice was raised, even in silence. It was then I learnt how various omission and restraint can be and learnt to admire and envy — indeed try to emulate — articulate silence."

I wonder if it isn't silence that comes hardest and ultimately, finally, between two people. Not the passive silence, even the first love contains that, but the active one. The silence that is neither unbearable or bearable but instead fluent, phatic. A silence of there-ness. How long can you maintain silence with anyone without losing yourselves to nervousness, anger, or confusion? An hour? A day? A week? A year?

It requires practice, and maybe it only available in a well-practiced routine, but I believe it to be possible, maybe not forever but for a little while.

1. Have you ever slept naked?
yes

2. Have you ever masturbated?
yes

3. What's your bra size, or dick length?
AA

4. Where was or would you want your first time to be and why?:
It was in a roof.

5. Have you ever gotten sexual with anything that wasn't a person?
no

6. Have you ever shown anyone your body parts and asked advice?
no

7. Have you ever seen any of your relatives naked?
yes

8 . Do you prefer doing it in the dark or in the light?

can you dim it?

9. What's your greatest fantasy?
I don't think I'm ever going to live down the washing machine one.

10. Would you suck on anyone's toes?
yeah if they wanted me to

11. Where do you think would be the weirdest place to have sex? :
inside a whale

12. Would you have sex there?
well if i was trapped in there and someone was up for it sure

13. How old do you think you'll be your first time?
ask me again four years ago

14. Would you ever have lesbian or gay sex?
yes

15. What do you think the sexiest fruit is?
tomato

16. Would you ever have an orgy with the same sex?
yes. no. maybe. that's nothing to do with 'same sex' tho

17. What and who turns you on?
one day they will invent technology that will allow someone to read my mind. that's all i can think of right now.

18. Have your hands ever been down anyone's pants?
yes

19. What superstar would you have sex with?

i bet radcliffe would be fun.

20. Have you or anyone else ever stuck anything down your pants?
yes

21. Have you ever had a dream about being gay or lesbian?
yes

22. Are you gay or lesbian?
no. but yes.

23. Whose the sexiest male or female you know?
wow jesus am i being triggered by these questions? i don't know :(

24. Have you ever made a guy get hard?
jake.
actually: not to my knowledge. feel free to anon if you want to tell me otherwise.

25. Have you ever counted your pubic hairs?
r u serious?

26. Would you rather be cute or sexy?
sexy

27. How many people would you have sex with at once?
0

28. Have you ever put on a strip show?
no

29. Have you ever seen a strip show?
no

30. Have you ever seen any of your friends naked?

yes

31. What's your kinky fetish?
people being horrible to me

32. Have you ever had a fantasy about a teacher?
yes

33. Have you ever had an orgasm?
yes

34. Have you ever gone skinny dipping?
no

35. Have you ever played with a condom?
yes

36. If you could be a spice what would it be?
celery salt

37. Would you use objects in sex such as whips, hand cuffs, etc.?
yeah

38. Have you ever tried on a condom?.
yes

39. Have you ever playfully spanked your lover?
no. yes, probably.

40. If someone says "spank me" do you do it and get turned on?
dunno, no.

41. Have you ever worn your underwear two days in a row?
yes

42. Have you ever seen anyone's dick?
yes

43. Have you ever compared your body parts to someone else's while you were both naked?
no

44. Have you ever took a piss standing up or squatting in the woods?
yes

45. What was the weirdest place you have ever done something with someone?
in a dilapidated house
(if you're reading, seb: yes, that house. i'm sorry.)
actually there's a weirder one. not saying.

46. What was the weirdest thing you have ever done to your b/f or g/f?
one time i breathplay'd my way to getting someone to pass out at the same time as they came.
don't try that at home please.

47. What was the worst thing your b/f or g/f did for you or to you?
okay, everyone reading this, just in case we ever end up sleeping together: don't touch my fucking balls. just don't. don't do it.

48. Have you ever wondered what position you would have sex in?
not really no

49. Have you ever used a vibrator on yourself or somebody else?
yes

50. Have you parents ever caught you doing anything?
no

51. Have you ever caught them?
no

52. Would you ever have sex in the ocean?
in the ocean? what's wrong with you? of cours enot

53. Have you ever gotten sand up you?
'up' me? no

54. Have you ever run or walked around your house nude?
yes

55. What do you wear to bed?
dad pyjamas. need a hat really

56. Have you ever done anything with someone in your own or parents bed?
in my own bed? yes. in my parents no

57. Would you ever consider rubbing hot oil or cream all over your guy or girl?
yeah if it was in their bed bc fuck cleaning that up

58. Have you ever eaten green M&M's?
...?

59. Have you ever used lubricant?
yes

60. Have you ever practiced kiss on something?
no

61. Have you ever fingered yourself, got fingered before or fingered someone else?

yes

62. Have you ever taken off your bra or underwear on a main road?
no

63. Would you ever do anything on a Ferris wheel?
yes, absolutely. i like being high up.

64. Have you ever given or received a hand job or blow job?
yes

65. What kitchen item would you label your b/f or g/f?
pizza cutter

66. Have you ever tasted cum or female juice?
lol 'female juice' i got a whole carton

67. What celebrity would you dip in hot chocolate?
jimmy carr. he wouldn't be coming out again, though.

68. What does the number "69" mean to you?
nothing at all

69. Have you ever played cops and robbers and if so what was your naughty crime?
no

71. What's the weirdest thing you can do with Jell-O?
probably fire it into space

72. Have you ever done anything with anyone in a pool, hot tub, or bath tub?
no

73. When you were little did you ever play with yourself?

yes

74. Have you ever tied up or hand cuffed anybody?
yes

75. Have you ever rested your head on somebody's chest or dick?
lol

77. Were you a witness to someone having sex?
no officer

78. Does ice cream turn you on?
yes

79. How about cherries?
no

80. Would you ever have phone sex?
no

81. Do you go by the rhythm of music?
no. but i like music to be around.

82. Would you ever do anyone in a tree?
yes

83. Would you ever have sexual contact with a relative?
no

84. Would you ever have sex with your best friend or someone you don't even know?
yes

85. Do you find physical pain like spanking an element of good sex?
yes

86. Do you find older women or men attractive?
not so often but sometimes

87. Would you rather have sex with or without a condom?
can't live with 'em, can't live without 'em

88. Who was the person you kissed that was the best?
redacted

89. If you had a half an hour to spend with your b/f or g/f what would you do?
ask em what's up

90. If you only had 20 minutes left to live what would you do?
i think about this a lot
1. write a facebook status saying goodbye.
2. message all my passwords to someone level. maybe grace
3. write a few messages to important people like my family, close friends
4. put a few names in a hat, pick one, call them and go out talking to them
5. turn off the lights

91. Which would you rather make out:
A) On a stage in front of a lot of people you know?
B) With your parents in the room?
C) In front of an ex?

A

92. Have you ever sneezed on your partner?
probably

93. What excuse would you give your parents if they

caught you having sex?
i'm 23 goddammit

94. Have you ever had a physical and how was it?
oh jesus

95. What color is your hair (pubic)?
dark, like you'd expect

96. Does your hair color match the color of your pubic hair?
yes

97. Have you ever opened your eyes while making out?
haha oh shit you got me

98. Your love life is like which of these movies:
A) Something about Mary
B) Chasing Amy
C) My Girl 2
D) When Harry Met Sally
E) Fatal Attraction (playa)
F) Rated X (not for young viewers)

i have seen none of those movies

99. Have you ever lost the keys to the cuffs or got stuck together?
no

100. Have you ever burped while making out?
no

101. Would you do anyone on your friends list?
uhhh yes

20

[y/n] snapped the novel shut and stopped breathing for a moment to test the silence. A car across the road has its door slammed. A shoe steps on newly drawn double-yeller lines and [y/n] is on their feet and walking quickly across the room to the window (they take the novel with them). They open the window and climb out taking a great but subtle effort to be quiet. They shut the window and sit down outside, waiting to hear what the figure does.

The figure knocks on the door, waits a minute, and then walks around like [y/n] hoped they would.

Because this house's garden, like the house of your childhood, has two exits. The first is the normal route around to the back door, and then there is another, narrower, exit. It is stopped up by compost and dead grass mostly but this only helps [y/n] by giving them something to step onto with a sort of springiness that helps them jump over the fence.

[y/n] crouches their legs slightly as they fall to absorb the impact. They had to do this consciously because they realised at some point that either that these things don't come naturally. They're not sure whether other people have to consciously crouch their legs this way but they know that they, [y/n], do. And so they do.

[y/n] checks their phone and sees that they have a bunch of notifications from tumblr about people liking their posts, people who have liked their posts before but who they don't know, which feels unusual but slightly flattering. Also one notification from gmail about work and one message from the NHS notifying them of an appointment being today and one message from someone they have a vaguely charged but non-sexual non-romantic relationship.

[y/n] opens the message from someone. it reads:

"These things take time. i'm seeing a lot of things twice lately. I need to work out my plans for the week. you ask too many questions."

[y/n] pressed the button on their phone and heard the echoey 'click' sound to indicate it was locked. "At least it's locked", they think. They think about responding to the message but they decide they will leave it until before bed to think about it for a while.

The figure is in their front room and is looking out. The figure has seen [y/n]!! [y/n] runs to their car and gets in and puts the keys into the engine (or presses the button) and pushes the clutch in and moves the gearstick to 'R' and finds the biting point and presses the accellerator and pulls off the clutch reverses too slowly out of the drive, turning the wheel to the.... left... anticlockwise and so getting into the road. Then they push the clutch in again and they switch to the '1' gear and find the biting point and then presses the accellerator and pulls off the clutch and drives away (they don't evne know how to drive! not really)

they're driving and driving and driving and the car is alll red. it's red not only on the outside but on the inside too, and the seats are red and the gearstick is red and the clutch is red. even the mirrors are red (but only tinted). and [y/n] is wearing a red jumper and also is a little embarrassed so they are also red. so when the figure drives past and looks into the car they can only see red and they drive past without seeing [y/n] at all. [y/n] thinks this is lucky and picks up the phone and sends a snapchat selfie of themselves in the red car with the red gearstick and the red clutch and the red-tinted mirrors and the red jumper and their red face. and they send it to everyone on their list which they don't do but it feels like a treat/self congratulation today. they feel a bit better but then they realise this will make their face not-red because they are not-embarrassed and so they keep thinking of embarrassing things to stay red. this is what they think of:

1. [y/n]'s earliest memory is of being by a fountain and looking around and people laughing at them and feeling confused and embarrassed. so they think of that
2. that time they had sex and it went wrong
3. that time their friend corrected them on what plaid was because they drew a distinction between checked and plaid and really checked is a kind of plaid? or something.
4. that time when someone was really crude and offhand to them in front of someone they were trying to impress and they didn't know what to do so they just acted really serious and vaguely 'consoling' which was inappropriate but
5. all the times they weren't introduced to someone despite being around
6. all that time they appropriated bits of text messages from an exchange with someone who might be reading and infer something from it

[y/n] decided to drive to france so they did. it didn't take very long and now they're in france. all the road signs are in french and the architecture and landscape is subtly different. then they drove back to England.

after this period of 'lying low' [y/n] thought they would return to their house and see what had happened there. they drove up and, being quite good at driving by this point, drove into the driveway with quite a lot of ease. they got out of their red car and they went to the door and they put their key in and opened the door and it opened under the pressure of their arm. there were five envelopes on the floor and this is what they said inside:

FIRST LETTER

YOUR NUMEROLOGICAL PERSONALITY AND FORECAST

Your birthdate and the name by which you are best known are the two most significant factors in the interpretation. The name you were given at birth, even if not presently used, also provides an important foundation in your life. These items, in various combinations and distillations, provide the basis for all the significant numbers found in your personal number chart.

THE INFLUENCE OF YOUR GIVEN NAME AT BIRTH

These are the characteristics encouraged by your parents and early upbringing. The subsequent change in your name indicates a modification or perhaps even a rejection of these early influences in favour of your own choices. Even if the change is only a minor one, such as a nickname or small spelling change, it is meaningful. Nevertheless, childhood influences have great significance and must be taken into consideration.

STEVEN adds up to 4. Such a person is basically honest, practical, hard-working and local. The number 4 is well-rganized and probably has mathematical talents and a good eye for detail. Such a person is intellectual in nature and exhibits a great mental endurance. There is a danger of becoming too rigid and dull despite a desire to break away from routine. A tendency to be methodical can make you a good problem solver as long as you don't sink too much into yourself and become moody or lonely.

THE INFLUENCE OF YOUR FAMILY NAME

Whether you changed your last name for a social reason, such as marriage, aesthetic, religious or other reasons, it indcates some desire to deviate, at least slightly, from the early influences or your original family structure. Nevertheless, the foundation established by the family at birth and during early childhood is significant and must be taken into consideration as part of the whole person.

THE INFLUENCE OF YOUR FAMILY NAME: BOOTH = 6

The number 6 family is usually very devoted to its home life and to extended family or community at large. These people are usually quite attractive, and may exhibit musical talent. In a negative atmosphere there may be too much emphasis on receiving the approval of others. The parets may be overly protective and interfere too much in their children's lives. When the atmosphere is positive, this family encourages service to the community that is also personally rewarding, and provides a sense of security and comfort in the home.

There may be a family medical history of allergies or problems in the lungs and chest.

THE INFLUENCE OF YOUR CURRENT LAST NAME

In some cultures it is common for married women to use their husbands' last names. There are other socially motivated reasons for changing one's last name, such as adoption or religious requirements. It is also more common than you may think for people to voluntarily decide to change their last names, perhaps as a symbolic gesture of some sort, separation from their family, aesthetic preferences, philosophical statement, or any number of other reasons. Practitioners of numerology may select names whose numbers indicate the path of change they wish to follow in their lives. No matter what your reason fro changing your name, it represents as strong present influence in your life and should be carefully studied.

THE INFLUENCE OF YOUR LAST NAME: LOVELACE = 3

People are attracted to your humor and charm. You may be attracted to a profession such as writing or music where you can fully develop your talent for self-expression. It's important not to let your joy of living in the moment lead to extravagance and carelessness. Remember to keep an eye on the future.

You probably appear younger than you are, and you can use this to your advantage in many ways. It's great fun for you to wear fashionable clothing and be socially popular, as long as you don't regress into immaturity.

THE INFLUENCE OF YOUR CURRENT FIRST NAME

The first name under which you are currently known has the ost influence over your life, particularly if it is the one that you chose for yourself, because it expresses not only your outward personality, but your inner aspirations.

CADEN adds up to 9. Its powers lie in strength of purpose, generosity and open-mindedness. Its weaknesses are false idealism, emotionalism, and aimlessness. The 9 has great potential for bettering the world. You will probably be drawn to one of the helping professions, where you can give unselfishly. You may tend to concentrate too much on the needs of others, thus neglecting your own health and safety. You can balance this tendency by remembering to direct some of your generosity and love towards yourself.

OTHER IMPORTANT ADVICE

In matters of love and marriage, it is important to remember that extreme opposites do not attract. At the same time, too much similarity can stifle growth in the relationship and can also limit you as an individual. Basic similarities and complementary differences are the key to balance.

Similar birth numbers, destiny numbers are considered important signs of compatibility. Additionally, you will find yourself attracted to people whose birth dates add up to 5 or 2. You will tend to have problems with those whose birth dates add up to 6 or 8.

Your style of loving may sometimes be considered unusual. You have a talent for surprise. Sunday and Wednesday are your energy days, and summer is your best season.

YOUR PLANES OF TEMPERAMENT AND POWER

Your name is highest on the PHYSICAL plane. Things that are tangible, physically real, have more meaning for you than things which seem metaphysical or imaginative. You have good physical endurance and well as mental stamina. Your nature is practical, probably leaning toward the conservative.

You have a good sense of responsibility, but you may become restless if your work seems too repetitive. You enjoy a change of pace now and then.

OTHER COMPONENTS OF YOUR CHARACTER

Your EXPRESSION number, 3, describes the combination of your first and last names, and thus gives and overall picture of the total you. This number will dominate over those of your PERSONALITY, 7, and INSTINCTIVE DESIRE, 5.

EXPRESSION: Three is a very cheerful number. Its positive traits are youthfulness, social skills, energy, and expressiveness. Its negative characteristics are gossip, hypocrisy, and false pride.

PERSONALITY: Seven is a highly spiritual number. Its positive traits are wisdom, inner awareness, logic, and an appreciation of nature. Seven's negative qualities are sarcasm, pessimism, and isolation.

DESIRE: Five is a number of great independence. Its positive traits are versatility, quick-mindedness, and a sense of adventure. Five's negative qualities are irresponsibility, carelessness and vulgarity.

YOUR DESTINY AND FORECAST NUMBERS

Your destiny and forecast numbers describe the lessons you need to learn n life and offer a view of situations that lie ahead. It is important to remember that a forecast is not a hard and fast prediction of events. The forecast indicates the most probable direction for you and the type of circumstnaces you are likely to face, given your overall character and traits.

Your ability to learn from experience, to anticipate situations and feelings, will allow you to make the most of the opportunities that come your way, and give you the chance to avoid or solve problems. With Numerology, you are not a helpless pawn of fate. Rather, your increased understanding and awareness allow you to take charge of your own destiny.

YOUR PERSONAL FORECAST FOR 2014

Your 2014 forecast number is 5, you may find yourself with an intense desire to make lots of changes in your life. Be careful not to let this urge drive you to make foolish choices. Let thelessons of your life experience guide you. The right changes can give you a wonderful new freedom. 2014 can be an exciting, dynamic year, as you open yourself to new experiences and new ideas. You might start a fitness program, move to a new home, embark on a new career, or travel far away. Your renewed interest in life will increase your personal attractiveness.

THE MASTER NUMBER 22 APPEARS IN YOUR READING:

This is a powerful number that affects you directly on the physical plane. It is sometimes called the Master Builder, because those who carry it can create enormous achievements in the world. The power can also be used for destruction rather than building, so you must be sure to exercise your best judgement as to the direction in which you will develop your strength.

22 is also a higher vibration of 4, a number that emphasiz-
es practical effort and loyalty.

YOUR LUCKY NUMBERS: 4 9 8 3 22

Your lucky colors are GRAY and BRIGHT BLUE.

[y/n] notes with a slight wonder and confusion that the CADEN
LOVELACE who has been profiled in this letter is the same name
as the person who wrote the novel that [y/n] was reading before
the figure arrived and that [y/n] is still carrying under their arm.

21

SECOND LETTER

It's irresistable, as a man, to place women into the positive stereotypes with which we have been taught to redeem femininity. The MPDG is an infamous one — 'positive' through and through, but complicit in our own masculine oppressive culture. The caring mother, the quiet-but-oversexed, the pure, the High Powered Professional Woman.

We see these, when we are men, as nuanced 'Individual' personalities. The not-like-the-other-girls. Attractive but not simple like the women on TV whose purpose is, and always has been, to be the simplest stereotypes for us to compare the complexities of real people to, so as to make their complexity more managable and positive for us, to make them 'unique' rather than...

...rather than face the terrifying fact that everyone is more complicated than we are able to cope with. rather than face the terrifying fact that all of your complexity and contingency is reduplicated within every person on earth and in space (they are there too, now).

AND, OUR SECOND LINE OF DEFENCE

And, our second line of defence, as men, is having boxed all of our positive feelings towards people, particularly women, into common cultural narratives. The saviour, the behind-every-great-man, the hot mess, the intellectual. All of these are vehicles to deny women their subjectivity and to make them unthreatening.

Ask a man, ask yourself, to describe in positive terms a woman who is close to you and you will hear your betrayal in your own voice, that is if you are capable of listening.

That is why men cannot ask women to love them, not women in general nor one woman in particular. Men, for decades and centuries have required, make legally compulsory, violently enforced the love of women for them to cover for the fact that it is impossible for a man to ask this of a woman, to expect it, to be righteous in their indignation when it is withdrawn. Men are the glass in the heels of women. To expect them to walk with us while with every step we betray them: it is clearly asinine.

There is a story:

Far, far from land, where the waters are as blue as the petals of the cornflower and as clear as glass, there, where no anchor can reach the bottom, live the mer-people. So deep is this part of the sea that you would have to pile many church towers on top of each other before one of them emerged above the surface.

Still, many evenings the five sisters would take each other's hands and rise up through the waters. They had voices far lovelier than any human being. When a storm began to rage and a ship was in danger of being wrecked, then the five sisters would swim in front of it and sing about how beautiful it was down at the bottom of the sea. They begged the sailors not to be frightened but to come down to them. The men could not understand the mermaids' songs; they thought it was the wind that was singing. Besides, they would never see the beauty of the world below them, for if a ship sinks the seamen drown, and when they arrive at the mer-king's castle they are dead.

On such evenings, while her sisters swam, hand in hand, up through the water, the youngest princess had to stay below. She would look sadly up after them and feel like crying; but mermaids can't weep and that makes their suffering even deeper and greater.

"Oh, if only I were fifteen," she would sigh. "I know that I shall love the world above, and the human beings who live up there!"

At last she, too, was fifteen!

At first, she thought joyfully, "Now he will come down to me!" But then she remembered that man could not live in the sea and the young prince would be dead when he came to her father's castle. "He must not die," she thought, and dived in among the wreckage, forgetting the danger that she herself was in, for any one of the great beams that were floating in the turbulent sea could have crushed her. She found him! He was too tired to swim any farther; he had no more strength in his arms and legs to fight the storm-whipped waves. He closed his eyes, waiting for death, and he would havedrowned, had the little mermaid not saved him. She held his head above water and let the waves carry them where they would.

"I know what you want," she cackled. "And it is stupid of you. But you shall have your wish, for it will bring you misery, little princess. You want to get rid of your fishtail, and instead have two stumps to walk on as human beings have, so that the prince will fall in love with you; and you will gain both him and an immortal soul." The witch laughed so loudly and evilly that the toad and eels she had had on her lap jumped down into the mud. "You came at the right time," she said. "Tomorrow I could not have helped you; you would have had to wait a year. I will mix you a potion. Drink it tomorrow morning before the sun rises, while you are sitting on the beach. Your tail will divide and shrink, until it becomes what human beings call 'pretty legs.' It will hurt; it will feel as if a sword were going through your body. All who see you will say that you are the most beautiful human child they have ever seen. You will walk more gracefully than any dancer; but every time your foot touches the ground it will feel as though you were walking on knives so sharp that your blood must flow. If you are willing to suffer all this, then I can help you."

"I will," whispered the little mermaid, and thought of her prince and how she would win an immortal

soul.

"But remember," screeched the witch, "that once you have a human body you can never become a mermaid again. Never again shall you swim through the waters with your sisters to your father's castle. If you cannot make the prince fall so much in love with you that he forgets both his father and mother, because his every thought concerns only you, and he orders the priest to take his right hand and place it in yours, so that you become man and wife; then, the first morning after he has married another, your

heart will break and you will become foam on the ocean."

"I still want to try," said the little mermaid, and her face was as white as a corpse.

"But you will have to pay me, too," grinned the witch. "And I want no small payment. You have the most beautiful voice of all those who live in the ocean. I suppose you have thought of using that to charm your prince; but that voice you will have to give to me. I want the most precious thing you have to pay for my potion. It contains my own blood, so that it can be as sharp as a double-edged sword." "But if you take my voice," said the little mermaid, "what will I have left?"

"Your beautiful body," said the witch. "Your graceful walk and your lovely eyes. Speak with them and you will be able to capture a human heart. Have you lost your courage? Stick out your lit-

tle tongue, and let me cut it off in payment, and you shall have the potion."

"Let it happen," whispered the little mermaid. The witch took out a caldron in which to make the magic potion. "Cleanliness is a virtue," she said. And before she put the pot over the fire, she scrubbed it with eels, which she had made into a whisk. She cut her chest and let her blood drip into the vessel. The steam that rose became strange figures that were terrifying to see. Every minute, the witch put something different into the caldron. When the brew reached a rolling boil, it sounded as though a crocodile were crying. At last the potion was finished. It looked as clear and pure as water.

"Here it is," said the witch, and cut out the little mermaid's tongue. Now she was mute, she could neither speak nor sing.

The sun had not yet risen when she reached the prince's castle and sat down on the lowest step of the great marble stairs. The moon was still shining clearly. The little mermaid drank the potion and it felt as if a sword were piercing her little body. She fainted and lay as though she were dead. When the sun's rays touched the sea she woke and felt a burning pain; but the young prince stood in front of her and looked at her with his coal-black eyes. She looked downward and saw then that she no longer had a fishtail but the most beautiful, little, slender legs that any girl could wish for. She was naked; and therefore she took her long hair and covered herself with it. The prince asked her who she was and how she had got there. She looked gently and yet ever so sadly up at him with her deep blue eyes, for she could not speak. He took her by the hand and led her up to his castle. And just as the witch had warned, every step felt as though she were walking on sharp knives. But she suffered it gladly. Gracefully as a bubble rising in the water, she walked beside the prince; and everyone who saw her wondered how she could walk so lightly.

"Don't you love me more than you do all others?" was the message in the little mermaid's eyes when the prince kissed her lovely forehead.

"Yes, you are the dearest to me," said the prince, "for you have the kindest heart of them all. You are devoted to me and you look like a young girl I once saw, and will probably never see again. I was in a shipwreck. The waves carried me ashore, where a holy temple lay. Many young girls were in service there; one of them, the youngest of them all, found me on the beach and saved my life. I saw her only twice, but she is the only one I can love in this world; and you look like her. You almost make her picture disappear from my soul. She belongs to the holy temple and, therefore, good fortune has sent you to me instead, and we shall never part."-"Oh, he does not know that it was I who saved his life,"thought the little mermaid. "I carried him across the sea to the forest where the temple stood. I hid behind the rocks and watched over him until he was found. I saw that beautiful girl whom he loves more than me!" And the little mermaid sighed deeply, for cry she couldn't. "He has said that the girl belongs to the holy temple and will never come out into the world, and they will never meet again. But I am with him and see him every day. I will take care of him, love him, and devote my life to him."

Everyone said that the young prince was to be married; he was to have the neighboring king's daughter, a beautiful princess. A magnificent ship was built and made ready. It was announced that the prince was traveling to see the neighboring kingdom, but that no one believed. "It is not the country but the princess he is to inspect," they all agreed. The little mermaid shook her head and smiled; she knew what the prince thought, and they didn't. "I must go," he had told her, "I must look at the beautiful princess, my parents demand it. But they won't force me to carry her home as my bride. I can't love her. She does not look like the girl from the temple as you do. If I ever marry, I shall most likely choose you, my little foundling with the eloquent eyes." And he kissed her on her red lips and played with her long hair, and let his head rest so near her heart that it dreamed of human happiness and an immortal soul.

"Are you afraid of the ocean, my little silent child?" asked the prince as they stood on the deck of the splendid ship that was to sail them to the neighboring kingdom. He told the little mermaid how the sea can be still or stormy, and about the fishes that live in it, and what the divers had seen underneath the water. She smiled as he talked, for who knew better than she about the world on the bottom of the ocean?

The little mermaid wanted ever so much to see her; and when she finally did, she had to admit that a more beautiful girl she had never seen before. Her skin was so delicate and fine, and beneath her long dark lashes smiled a pair of faithful, dark blue eyes.

"It is you!" exclaimed the prince. "You are the one who saved me, when I lay half dead on the beach!" And he embraced his blushing bride. "Oh, now I am too happy," he said to the little mermaid. "That which I never dared hope has now happened! You will share my joy, for I know that you love me more than any of the others do." The little mermaid kissed his hand; she felt as if her heart were breaking. His wedding morning would bring her death and she would be changed into foam of the ocean.

"We have given our hair to the sea witch, so that she would help you and you would not have to die this night. Here is a knife that the witch has given us. Look how sharp it is! Before the sun rises, you must plunge it into the heart of the prince; when his warm blood sprays on your feet, they will turn into afishtail and you will be a mermaid again. You will be able to live your three hundred years down in the sea with us, before you die and become foam on the ocean. Hurry! He or you must die before the sun rises. Our grandmother mourns; she, too, has no hair; hers has fallen out from grief. Kill the *prince and come back to us! Hurry! See, there is a pink haze on the horizon. Soon the sun will rise and you will die." The little mermaid heard the sound of her sisters' deep and strange sighing before they disappeared beneath the waves.*

She pulled aside the crimson cloth of the tent and saw the beautiful bride sleeping peacefully, with her head resting on the prince's chest. The little mermaid bent down and kissed his handsome forehead. She turned and looked at the sky; more and more, it was turning red. She glanced at the sharp knife; and once more she looked down at the prince. He moved a little in his sleep and whispered the name of his bride. Only she was in his thoughts, in his dreams! The little mermaid's hand trembled as it squeezed the handle of the knife, then she threw the weapon out into the sea. The waves turned red where it fell, as if drops of blood were seeping up through the water. Again she looked at the prince; her eyes were already glazed in death. She threw herself into the sea and felt her body changing into foam.

This too, is a betrayal.

THIRD LETTER

The third letter was blank.

FOURTH LETTER

The fourth letter was blank

FIFTH LETTER

This is the end, [y/n]. The last four-hundred words.
I've decided, in fact, to make this novel 49,999 words. I don't
know why, and I know that, [y/n], as you're reading this, you'll feel
like this is a bit weak. And I really don't have much of a defence to
this, but— I don't know, there's something about almostness that
always gets me. And really, if you prefer, you can decide that this
novel is over 50k words because counting words is an imprecise
science really. But...
...in that last story, about the mermaid. There is an ending that
isn't that one. She becomes a spirit of the airs and gets a chance
to earn her soul by doing good deeds for 300 years. But, I, and I
gather some other historians, consider this a bit weak, and in fact
unnatural, like it was tacked on for some reason. And why would
it be tacked on? He lost his nerve, perhaps, or someone demanded
it of him. I don't know. Perhaps he didn't even write it. The story
or the ending.
[y/n], I feel amazed that we are here.
[y/n], I'm happy you're here with me.
[y/n],
I'm going to make a bagel.

[y/n] folds the letters up and puts them on the side on the table
on the side. She ascends the stairs and climbs onto the windowsil
and falls out. She goes back around and back in the door and past
the letters, and she does this a few more times and eventually she
makes it out onto the roof by a process of twisting her body further than she feels it ought to go. [y/n] is on the roof. It starts to
rain. [y/n] recieves a snapchat on her phone and it is of a horse.
Another one is of the sunset somewhere far away. Another one is
just gray. The rain is all on her screen and it's making the pixels
decompose and be all coloursy and bulbous. [y/n] receives a text
message. It reads:

"Hi, get a free £20 bet on Chelsea v Man City when

Let's be very careful. Let's prepare ourselves. A sudden break now, however brave and admirable will be too cruel. We can't do such violence to our hearts and minds.

People who are in this to varying degrees:

Alex Goodman, Blare Coughlin, Chloë Smith, Gionna Rose, Grace Thomas, Ian Aleksander Adams, Italo Calvino, Izzy Khan, Jack Serge, Jerome Fletcher, Jesse Darling, Jessica Johnson, John Hall, Jojo McCourt, Marie Calloway, Penny Goring, Rachael Clerke, Scarlett Lassoff, Steve Roggenbuck (sorry), Tao Lin, that guy who said we will not know freedom as long as there is grammar, Wal-Mart Stores, Inc., @horse_ebooks (deceased).

Thanks.